Just 'Cause He Won Her, Didn't Mean He Had to Keep Her!

"There's maybe some confusion that will want studying out," he said finally. "I'll go downstairs and do some figuring on it. You just turn in, all right?"

She made no protest, merely said, "Fine," and, seating herself on the bed, pulled out some pins and let her pale blonde hair uncoil and fall down her back.

"I couldn't say just when I'll be back up," Faro said.

Rosa nodded and began unbuttoning the front of her bodice.

"It might just be better if I bunked down somewheres else until everything's sorted out," Faro said .

Rosa stood, pushed the unbuttoned dress down and stepped out of it.

"Well, I'll be going," Faro said hoarsely.

Rosa pulled the camisole off over her head and dropped it on the bed.

"Uh, be seeing you," Faro managed to get the door open, back out of the room and close it.

He pushed the door open again. "Don't believe I'll go down to the bar just now."

"Didn't think you would."

Books by Zeke Masters

The Big Gamble
Bottom Deal
Diamond Flush
Four of a Kind
Luck of the Draw
Riverboat Showdown
Threes Are Wild

Published by POCKET BOOKS

#7

A ZEKE MASTERS WESTERN

BOTTOM DEAL

PUBLISHED BY POCKET BOOKS NEW YORK

Another *Original* publication of POCKET BOOKS

POCKET BOOKS, a Simon & Schuster division of
GULF & WESTERN CORPORATION
1230 Avenue of the Americas, New York, N.Y. 10020

ISBN: 0-671-42618-4

First Pocket Books printing June, 1981

10 9 8 7 6 5 4 3 2 1

POCKET and colophon are trademarks of Simon & Schuster.

Printed in the U.S.A.

BOTTOM DEAL

Chapter 1

Faro Blake lounged against the deck railing of the *Gulf Flyer* and watched the coastal packet's walking beams shudder into motion. It galled him to be leaving Galveston so hurriedly, but, all things considered, it was a good idea. . . .

A *damned* good idea, he amended inwardly as a hoarse shout of *"Blake!"* from behind him sent him swiveling around. A massive, dark-clad figure stood on the dock with two revolvers leveled at him. One belched flame from its muzzle, and a splinter flew from the railing, inches from where his back rested on it.

Faro dove for the shelter of a stack of cotton bales against the railing as the shoreside gunman continued his fusillade. Faro watched the walking beams pick up speed and calculated that the ship would soon be out of pistol range from the pier.

"Now, there's the hand of Providence for you," a

fellow passenger said, crouched alongside Faro. "You could of been standing aft instead of forward when that fellow started loosing off at you, and ducked behind the deck cargo *there* instead of *here*," the man said.

"And?"

"Which that's black powder for blasting."

The protective cotton bale shuddered as another slug bit into it; so did Faro.

The other passenger eyed him, taking in the long black coat and narrow-cut trousers, the ruffled white shirt-front punctuated with diamond studs, the narrow string tie, and the broad-brimmed black hat, as well as the habitually wary, wide-cheekboned face and narrowed greenish eyes.

"Would size you up as a gambling man?" he said. At Faro's curt nod he continued: "That fellow with the artillery, did he take a notion that you won when you shouldn't of?"

"In a manner of speaking," Faro said.

Faro studied his one remaining opponent. Blanton had stayed in when the others had folded, so he had to have something respectable. But the last raise had plainly pretty well cleared him out; he'd had to search in three pockets before he came up with the needed cash. Faro suspected that Blanton had got himself into that most dangerous of all frames of mind for a gambler, feeling that he *had* to win this one. Once a man convinced himself of that, it's not much of a step to persuading himself that Lady Luck will bless his mingy two pair and make them, for once, a winning hand.

Faro's relationship with Lady Luck was respectful but distant. They had had some damned good times in the past, and likely would again, but she was nobody to rely on for day-to-day business. For that, he went with the odds, and they said that his four sevens would beat more hands than it would lose to. And his experience—nearly twenty-five years of it now, going back to the riverboat days when he was twelve—told him that a man holding sure-fire winning cards didn't have to make the effort Blanton was to keep his face expressionless.

He shoved coins to the center of the table, matching Blanton's raise. "I'll call."

Blanton looked hopeful as he laid down his ace-high full house, then crestfallen at the sight of Faro's hand. The players who had dropped out—a couple of cattlemen from up toward the Indian Territory, a Louisiana planter, and a tall man someone had said was a Texas Ranger—murmured appreciatively.

"Unless one of you gentlemen'd care to go on, I'd as soon call it a night," Faro said. The evening's poker session in the ornate Grand Saloon of the Galveston House had been pleasant enough—and satisfactorily profitable for Faro—but there had been no spectacular wins or losses, and he suspected that the erstwhile players would prefer to drift over to the hotel's well-stocked bar to finish off the day's recreation.

Only Blanton demurred. "You've got to give me a chance to win something back," he said. "You can't just close up like that. One more hand, just you and me, if nobody else'll join in."

Faro sighed and studied him. Blanton was a good-looking man in his mid-twenties, a little heavy under the chin, elegantly dressed. If pressed to identify his trade, Faro would have said actor, except that in his experience an actor would usually let you know right away what he'd been playing in, why he was now "resting," and what Edwin Booth or Jo Jefferson had once said to him. All the same, there was something theatrical—artificial, maybe—about Blanton. In any case, if he insisted on playing, Faro had a professional obligation to accommodate him. If, that is, he had the wherewithal. . . .

"No disrespect," Faro said, "but I got to tell you, I don't take markers."

Blanton glowered at him, then said, "But it doesn't have to be a cash stake, does it? I mean, a gold watch or something, you'd let a man put that in the pot for its value?"

"In a pinch," Faro said warily.

Blanton rose, turned and gestured at a figure seated at the far side of the room. In response, a woman rose and approached the table as Blanton resumed his seat. The spectators stirred and Faro's eyes widened as she leaned over to address Blanton, her low-cut dress revealing a substantial portion of a smooth and shapely bosom. "Yes, honey?" she said in a soft voice that gave Faro the impression that she had been drinking cream—which fit the general impression she made, as she seemed to him to resemble nothing so much as a large, pampered house cat he'd once seen in a Kansas City bordello: soft, sinuous, and silky.

"Could you tell me the time, Rosa?" Blanton said.

The woman dipped a slender hand into the deep cleft between her breasts and fetched up an enameled watch on the end of a chain, then studied it. So did Faro, estimating its worth at about twenty dollars, and wondering how Blanton was going to explain that he was about to hazard her property in a poker game.

"Minute or so past ten," the woman said.

"Thanks. I'll be through here in a few minutes; you go on back there," Blanton said. The woman nodded, smiled vaguely at Faro and the standing spectators, and returned to her place.

"Now, what's that worth?" Blanton said.

"The watch? Well, I didn't get a close look, but—"

"You got a close enough look at what matters," Blanton cut in. "I'm not staking any gimcrack watch, Blake. It's Rosa that's going in the pot!"

"The hell she is," Faro said. "You can't ante up your wife—"

"Not my wife, just my woman. So there's nothing wrongful to it. One night with Rosa, you saw something of what she's like, dressed—I'll tell you, when the stays come off, she's something you wouldn't believe."

"Now, that is some sporting offer, Blake," one of the ranchers said. "I believe I would like to see that game played. Would give a pretty to be there when you rake in the pot, if so as you win."

Faro eyed Blanton sourly. He hated freak bets and unpredictable losers, but the spectators were clearly in favor of the bizarre stake—he couldn't refuse to accept it and retain the credit his trade demanded. He meant to stay in Galveston for a few months until the hot weather set in, then cut out for the milder climates of San Francisco or Seattle, and couldn't afford to get a name for shunning play.

And what the hell. The woman was undeniably first-rate goods, and collecting—as, with this player, he had no doubt he would—would be a lot more interesting than raking in a handful of bills and coins.

"I don't know as our paths will cross again," Faro said to Blanton, "but whether you're playing against me or another gambler, I will tell you, don't ever draw to a inside straight."

11

"I thank you for the advice," Blanton said, less daunted by his loss than Faro had expected. "I'll go tell Rosa to be at your room by midnight. Unless," he added, "you'd care to reconsider and offer something for a longer arrangement? I have the feeling I could beat you, the next hand."

Faro refused firmly, and Blanton went over to Rosa.

"Took his loss like a man," the Louisiana planter said approvingly.

"Well, it's a slice out of a cut loaf, you might say," one of the ranchers commented. "It ain't so much a loss as a lend." He, the other rancher and the planter departed for the bar.

Faro gathered up the cards and looked over toward where Blanton was bending to talk to Rosa, partly expecting to see her fetch him a good clout with her reticule; but no, as far as Faro could tell, she was taking the news as calmly as she'd given Blanton the time, earlier.

"It's a while 'til the clock racks up the dozen and my stack of chips over there wanders on up to be cashed in," he said to the tall Ranger. "Buy you a drink?"

"So you had this fellow sitting a horse, noose around his neck and snubbed over a tree limb and invited him to talk, huh?" Faro said, as they sat at the bar. "Expect he confided pretty readily?"

Reid nodded. "Told us where the gang was holed up and all."

"And then?"

Reid shrugged. "My sergeant hit the horse a lick and it ran off."

"Uh," Faro said uneasily, "you mean . . ."

"That sort of operation," Reid said, "there's not much taking of prisoners. There was only three of us, and at least eight left in the gang. Couldn't spare anyone to guard him, so . . . Besides," he added, "something like that now and then, it's wonderful what it does for the Rangers' reputation. The word gets around that it doesn't pay to mess with even a few Rangers—or only one, if it comes down to that."

Faro could agree with the logic of this—nothing in his plans called for crossing Reid or any other Ranger, but he would certainly be restudying any such idea if he'd had it—but decided it was time for a change of subject. "You got any relations in the gunsmith trade?" he asked.

"Not that I know of."

"Reason I ask," Faro said, "is that a man same name as yours made this, which has been useful to me many's the time." He fetched out his knuckle-duster/pistol from a vest pocket and showed it to the Ranger. "Reid, yes," the Ranger said, reading the maker's name engraved on the butt, "but no kin, far as I'm aware. Doesn't look up to much," he added, inspecting the short barrel and the ringed grip that allowed the weapon to double as a set of brass knuckles.

"Doesn't have to be," Faro said. "When a disagreement comes up in my line of work, it's a close-up kind of business, and the big thing is to have something right to hand; and this one I can use as a shooter or as something less permament, depending as is called for."

"That all you carry?" Reid wanted to know.

"These clothes, there wouldn't be room for much more," Faro said. He could have added, but did not, that when he anticipated substantial trouble, it was his custom to sling inside his frock coat a shotgun, butt

13

and barrel cut down so drastically that the weapon was little larger than an old-fashioned dragoon's pistol, though it packed a punch lethal to anything living at up to thirty feet and standing even approximately where it was pointed. It now rested, with his faro box and layout, and the selection of "advantage tools" he carried always—not that he had any intention of running a rigged game, but it was plain foolish not to be able to if the necessity arose—in the brass-fitted leather case in his room upstairs. He had found it good policy not to mention this second weapon too freely. It was the kind of thing that was best used as a surprise, and a surprise that people know about isn't much of one.

Reid favored him with a few more stories of law enforcement as he had known—and evidently enjoyed —it, then seemed to sense something of Faro's private opinion, that Quantrill's raiders could have learned something from the Rangers. "You got to understand," Reid said, "that we're not dealing with the usual run of people, as you might get in New York, 'Frisco, Dodge, places like that. A man in law enforcement, usually he figures he's got ninety-five out of a hundred of the local people on his side, so it's the other five he's got to pay attention to. But in Texas, it doesn't work that way. There's the Indians, that don't see why anybody else should be here, and don't count it more than a little amusement to kill, torture, maim, or anything else that occurs to them; and then there's the Mexicans, that ain't got used to Texas not being Mexican any more and don't see that the treaty of Guadalupe Hidalgo binds them to any kind of civilized dealings; and, worst of all, you've got the Texians, folks that came in from the States, turned the whole

14

damn place into a Republic, then got it grafted onto the U.S., and then by God did what they could to get it out again when they joined the Confederacy. Indian, Mex or Anglo, anybody that's been in Texas any amount of time has about the hardest noses a human can grow. And if there's to be any law at all, it's going to come out of the muzzle of a Ranger's six-shooter, which in the nature of things doesn't leave much room for writs of mandamus or reversals on appeal."

"You occupied with anything like that just now?" Faro asked.

"On leave," Reid answered. "Supposed to be a week before I report back, but I doubt I'll get all my time in. Haven't had a full leave in close to ten years, usually happens that something boils up, and General Steele up in Austin figures that it's right up John Reid's alley, and gets on the telegraph, telling me to get to wherever it is and improvise. That's the thing of it—I got a name for improvising, which I had to do to stay alive in some bad scrapes, so it works out that when something comes along that's out of the general run and they're not sure what to do, they figure I'll improvise my way out of it. So I get pitchforked into worse scrapes than ever. I get fed up with it sometimes, but Rangering is the only kind of work I know, and I don't see that it's the kind of business you can set up in on your own."

"Whereas mine is," Faro said. "It does have its peculiarities, though. I have won fellows' watches and horses, and once a deed to some bottom land, but the usage of a woman is a new kind of pot for me."

"At least it's not a situation where you'll have to improvise too much," Reid said.

"I will say I have the requirements pretty well

15

studied out by now," Faro said. "Less have another couple drinks."

Upstairs in his room an hour later, Faro stowed his cash winnings and settled down to await the enjoyment of his more lively prize.

It was just at midnight that the knock came. Faro went to the door of the room and opened it.

"Mr. Blake?" Blanton's companion stood in the doorway, smiling at him composedly. She was every bit as luscious as he remembered, and he found himself responding to her sensuous appeal with a sudden and unmistakable physical manifestation. . . . Which dwindled suddenly as he caught sight of the large valise she held awkwardly in one hand.

Chapter 2

"That's what Mr. Blanton told me," Rosa was explaining a few moments later, to Faro's mounting consternation. "That he had to leave Galveston real sudden on a matter of business, and that I was to stay with you until he sent for me. He paid up at the rooming house where we were and took me on over here, said goodbye and tipped his hat to me, then went off."

"Did he say was he going to the train station or what?" Faro asked, though he was dismally aware that Blanton, having deftly dumped his inamorata, was not likely to have left a trail that could be quickly followed—by now, he would be almost anywhere in Galveston, or on his way out of it.

"I didn't ask," Rosa said. "He said you would see to me as long as was needful."

"Well, I . . ." Faro paused. There had to be a kindly way to tell this poor woman that she had been abandoned callously, but he couldn't quite figure what it might be. Also, he wasn't sure that even if he were to put it to her bluntly, the message would get through. Back in the saloon, she had reminded him of a giant cat, and she was now displaying a cat's calm assumption of welcome and nurture. It would probably take, he reflected, a boot flung at her head to move her now. One thing was sure, any notion of a frolic on the sheets was off. Rosa was no longer a prize—shit, he cursed inwardly, I *knew* the sonofabitch threw the game!—but a responsibility. He'd have to figure out what to do about her, maybe tomorrow find a respectable landlady for her to stay with while he worked out the best answer. Tonight, she could have the bed, and he'd sit up in the armchair—no, he'd go back down to the bar and prime his brain with a little more bourbon, let her have the room all to herself. Attractive though she was, she left him totally cold right now.

"There's maybe some confusion that will want studying out," he said finally. "I'll go downstairs and do some figuring on it. You just turn in, all right?"

She made no protest, merely said, "Fine," and, seating herself on the bed, pulled out some pins and let her pale-blonde hair uncoil and fall down her back.

"I couldn't say just when I'll be back up," Faro said.

Rosa nodded and began unbuttoning the front of her bodice. As it gaped, it exposed a thin camisole—not much more than a film of cloth—covering the sumptuous breasts that had made such a powerful impression on him when she had leaned over Blanton at the table.

"It might just be better if I bunked down some-wheres else until everything's sorted out," Faro said.

Rosa stood, pushed the unbuttoned dress down, and stepped out of it. Her drawers were a little more sub-stantial than the camisole, but not much; her creamy flesh seemed to glow through them, and through the silk stockings that encased her thighs and calves, upheld by pale-blue garters, vanishing into small, light-tan shoes.

"Well, I'll be going," Faro said hoarsely.

Rosa pulled the camisole off over her head and dropped it on the bed. The enameled watch, tangled in the doffed garment, dropped back askew, its chain ringing her left breast, under which it dangled, light from the lamp winking on it.

"Good night, then," Faro said. He felt behind him for the doorknob, and wondered vaguely why it was so slippery in his grasp.

Rosa reseated herself on the bed, pulled off her shoes, unfastened her garters and carefully drew her stockings off. Faro could feel what seemed to be three separate pulses pounding in his throat, chest, and groin. "You'll be all right?"

"Fine." She stood again, slipped her thumbs into the waistband of her drawers, and slid them down and stepped out of them. She flexed her arms and arched her back, stretching in a gesture that reminded Faro even more strongly of a cat—though no cat had ever had the effect on him that Rosa was, once more, bringing about. "I like nice clothes, but it's good to get out of them, they pinch and bind so." Rosa scratched absently at her waist, which bore the fading reddish marks of her dress's tight fit.

"Uh, be seeing you," Faro managed to say, getting a grip on the doorknob and turning it.

He got the door open, backed out of the room, and closed it. He ran a damp hand across his damp forehead. Rosa's casual undressing, and what it had displayed, had damn near been enough to undo his resolution to stay clear of her until he had settled what was to become of her. The last thing he needed was an entanglement with a woman who evidently had no notion of fending for herself but calmly assumed that there'd be a warm bed and a saucer of cream—or whatever it was she fancied—set out for her wherever she cared to light.

Once he had arranged it so that she wasn't his responsibility, things might be different, of course. That would be the time, if any, to explore the delights offered by those rounded, firm thighs and what lay between them at the honey-colored patch of hair under the gently swelling belly, those pale, full lips, those pink-pointed breasts that swayed with every movement . . .

He pushed the door open. "Don't believe I'll go down to the bar just now."

"Didn't think you would." She was lying face-down on the bed, her upper body raised up on her elbows, lightly stroking one forearm. Her body glowed in the lamplight, and her hair fell in a golden spray down her back.

Faro shed his clothes with fumbling haste, scattering them on the floor as he crossed the room. She flexed her knees and rose up on all fours to meet him as he scrambled onto the bed.

The touch of her flesh was cool against his loins as he entered her in one long, urgent thrust, cool on his hands as he cupped her breasts, savoring their softness punctuated by the stiffly puckered nipples.

He had feared that Rosa would be placid and un-

responsive—willing enough, sure, but ready to let him
do whatever he had a mind to without getting
involved in it. But, under him, she was lithe and responsive, moving with a sureness of instinct or practice that brought him to the point of climax almost
immediately, then held him there for delirious minutes. Her back and flanks were slick and glistening
with sweat now, and a musky scent rose from her
body and from her hair, some of which lay plastered
to her back, the rest of it hanging beside or in front
of her face like a mane. Her fingers splayed out on
the bedclothes, kneading them almost in rhythm with
his thrusts.

Suddenly she arched her back and partially withdrew from him, yet somehow clenched to grip him
still tighter. He looked down and saw the swollen
length of his cock protruding from her, then drove in
again, hard but slow against her moist constriction,
and felt himself coming even as he completed the
thrust.

They collapsed in a damp tangle, breathing in
deep, shuddering gasps. After a few moments, Faro
wondered what to say. "Thank you, that was real
fine," didn't seem to fit, certainly accurate though it
might be. Any way, Rosa didn't seem much inclined
to polite conversation.

He supported himself on one elbow and, with the
other hand, traced the length of her spine with a slow,
stroking motion. She moved appreciatively under his
touch and uttered a throaty "Mmmm." It had the
quality of a purr.

"Well, it was foolish, I know that, but Mr. Schofield
was so kind of strict, and Mr. Blanton was so hand-

some and gentlemanly, that I just found myself going off with him when he asked me."

Rosa was curled comfortably on the bed, head nested on the pillow; Faro sat in the armchair. The night was warm, and neither had seen any reason to resume any clothing. They were both sipping from tumblers of bourbon which Faro had poured from his traveling flask.

Rosa seemed neither regretful of what she called her foolishness nor—as some women might be—proud of it, as lending distinction to her personality. She was the way she was and, give her credit, knew and accepted it, Faro thought. She was foolish in the same way she was blonde or, as now, splendidly naked, and was equally unself-conscious about all her characteristics.

Faro now had at least one hard fact: she was lawfully married to a man named Schofield. It wasn't the time to press her for details, but it seemed to him that the thing to do in the morning would be to find out from her where this Schofield lived, then set about discovering if he wanted his wife back. Considering her talents, he'd be a damned fool if he didn't, so long as he could work out a way to keep her reasonably well corralled.

"It's not in me to say no when someone's nice to me," Rosa said thoughtfully. "I expect that's why Mr. Schofield was so strict, but that made Mr. Blanton seem all the nicer when he made up to me, didn't it? So being strict didn't work out well, when you come down to it. Mr. Schofield will be awful vexed over this, but he really needn't be. He's not as gentlemanly as Mr. Blanton, but he's *better*."

"Uh . . . churchgoing man?" Faro said, surprised

that Rosa should dwell on her abandoned husband's moral qualities.

"No. I mean, Mr. Blanton, he'd take his pleasure, and that'd be it. He wouldn't be interested again until the morning, and after that not until night. There wouldn't be anything *steady* about it."

"Mr. Schofield's different in that respect, huh?" Faro asked, quickly revising his mental picture of a sternly puritanical spouse for Rosa.

"Oh, my, yes." Rosa sipped her drink and gave a dreamy smile. "He'd pleasure himself and me, then he'd pleasure me and I'd pleasure him and so on. Some nights we'd get a little short on sleep, but it seemed to me that what we got was so deep that it made up. And of course there was the mornings, and it usually happened he could get home for lunch. He had to be out of town on his work for close to a week, though, and I suppose that's how it came about that I paid attention to Mr. Blanton. He has rich folks, he said, and travels for them on business, though I will say I never saw him doing any."

Faro guessed that he'd be pretty close to the mark in pegging Blanton as a remittance man—a black-sheep member of a prominent family paid a meager allowance as long as he stayed far, far away from the ancestral home.

He also realized that he had developed a profound respect for Rosa's husband. The man might be short on gentlemanliness, but he must have the endurance and enthusiasm of a stallion. Faro suspected that he himself had been rated better on Rosa's scale than Blanton, but that he fell far short of Schofield's standard of performance. Right now, for instance, he was totally played out, and the voluptuous display of Rosa, creamy, gold and pink, curled on the bed, moving sinuously now and then to get even more comfortable, couldn't rouse so much as a twitch in him.

Well, maybe a twitch—he took another sip of bourbon and let the warmth trickle down his gullet and reach toward his groin—but only a little twitch, nothing you could . . .

"Mmm," Rosa said, eyeing him. She slid from the bed and crossed to him, then crouched in front of him. She reached out a pale hand and ran a sharp pink-tinted fingernail up the side of his barely responsive penis. It was like a delicate caress from a claw, a needle-fine line of near-pain from root to head, and it brought him to full erectness instantly.

She smiled, revealing sharp, even teeth, and bent forward to him, nuzzling his legs apart. He was expecting the moist engulfment of her mouth, but instead received a series of gentle nips up the length of his shaft. He was about to protest, "Hey, that hurts!" then realized it didn't—that it was so strongly arousing that he had to will himself to keep from coming right then. Which would be a damned waste, he considered, as Rosa, once more smiling, slid back from him to lie full-length on the carpet.

He was out of the chair, onto her and into her in one swift movement. He wondered distractedly which had been better, the first time, mounting her for that fantastic ride from above, or this one, face to face, catching the play of expression and the gyrations of her breasts as she twisted and thrust beneath him— then he decided that comparisons didn't matter worth a damn.

Faro was careful not to waken Rosa when he left the room in the morning. A little A.M. loving was a fine thing—or a lot of it, likely, considering he was dealing with Rosa—but he would need some refueling before he was up to it. With a moderate breakfast in him—say a steak, a couple of eggs, biscuits and red gravy, a pot or so of coffee—he ought to be able to do her justice. And a dozen oysters wouldn't be a bad idea, either.

In the hotel's dining room, he got the waiter started on his order, added a plate of fried potatoes as an afterthought, and set to work. When the second pot of coffee came and the array of empty dishes had been cleared, his ravenousness had been dispelled, but in its place there came a gnawing worry.

No question, Rosa was as prime a woman as he recalled laying leg over, but fucking wasn't the whole of life. There was gambling and drinking, for instance, and a man would have to stay in tip-top shape, no serious boozing or habitual late hours, if he meant to make a steady thing of her. Plenty of fresh air and strenuous exercise, and four or five solid meals a day. So a man whose custom it was to rise nearer noon than dawn and breakfast on an egg beaten up in brandy, whose lungs felt scratchy if there weren't enough tobacco smoke in the air—a man like that had no business taking up with Rosa.

From her account, Schofield had been just the ticket, and now, having sampled the field, she might be more inclined to value him and respect what she called his strictness. It seemed to him that it might be a poor idea to question Rosa too closely until his plans were firmed up; so the problem was, where to locate a man named Schofield somewhere in Texas?

He puffed a thin cigar moodily as he calculated his chances of doing this. Then he brightened. In the doorway of the dining room, he saw Reid, the Ranger captain—just the man to know how to go about locating an elusive stranger.

Reid, he saw, was talking to a burly man, a near-giant, with a broad face red with anger or the outdoors. In spite of his sober, expensive-looking suit—which had to be tailor-made, considering his massive frame—the man looked dangerous. Faro left his table and approached the pair, but hung back until their conversation seemed to be ending.

The big man started to lumber away, then turned and said, "Good luck, John. You'll need it."

"Expect I will," Reid said, creasing a slip of buff paper that looked to Faro like a telegram and slipping it into his vest pocket. "If I don't find it, I'll have to make it, but I'm used to that. And good luck to you, Ben, with your . . ."

"Yeah!" the man said savagely, and strode away.

"Join me for coffee, Captain?" Faro asked.

Reid gave him an amused look and said, "Yeah."

"Run into a friend just now?" Faro asked, pouring the Ranger a mug of coffee.

"Colleague, sort of. Marshal of a town over near Arkansas, here on private business."

"Looked like a hardcase," Faro observed. He emptied his own mug and began to refill it.

"Got to be. He's one of these fellows a town calls in when things have got so rough that they can't be handled and for one reason or another it doesn't turn out to be Ranger business. Like Earp or Hickock, say—shows 'em all he's more dangerous than the worst bad man, and things quiet down wonderfully. But Earp and Hickock don't hardly rate for poison-pure toughness alongside Ben Schofield. You figuring to dye that tablecloth brown? You're pouring coffee all over it."

A waiter, clucking with disapproval, hurried over

and replaced the sodden tablecloth, bringing another pot of coffee and, at Faro's insistence, a bottle of brandy.

When he had fortified his coffee with this and taken a gulp, Faro said flatly, "Private business?"

Reid nodded, smiling slightly. "His wife ran off with a drifter a while back, and he traced them to Galveston. He aims to bring her back home, with maybe an ear or whatever off the remains of the drifter as a souvenir, to remind her not to stray."

"That man Blanton last night," Faro said. "And his woman, the one he——"

"Figured it might be them," Reid said, "but it wasn't my business. He'll likely turn them up wherever they're staying—I take it the lady'll be back there by now, having paid off on Blanton's stake?"

Faro urgently explained the changed situation.

"Well, he won't find Blanton," Reid said. "But in a while he'll find Mrs. S. *and* you, looks like, and won't see any reason not to use you as a stand-in for Blanton. The lesson'd be the same either way. You want to change the upshot, I would say you'd have to vamoose pretty quick. The day staff at the hotel here won't know about Mrs. S., but when Ben comes back in the afternoon and asks the night shift, somebody'll probably remember seeing her go up to your room last night. You figure to take her with you?"

Faro shook his head. "I don't feel I got a right to stand between a man and his wife, which in this case it would be like standing between a hammer and an anvil. I am on my own from here. But the thing is, I got no idea where to go. All the places I know hereabouts are pretty fair-sized towns, and I light in any one of them, this Schofield is likely to hear of me and come hot-foot to disarrange me."

"True enough," Reid said. "It might be seen as letting Ben down, but I don't hold you to blame in this, you not knowing the lady was married, so I will give you a tip. Head for West Texas—it's still frontier out there, and a natural refuge for a man to go that doesn't want to be heard of for a while. Wild sort of place, but one where questions aren't much asked. I know of a town, San Bernardo, a good ways up the Rio Grande—you get yourself over there, and I doubt you'll be concerned about Ben Schofield again."

He suggested that Faro take a coastwise steamer and get off at Port Isabel, at the mouth of the Rio Grande, where he could get passage on an upstream packet that would land him at San Bernardo. "That way, should Ben get on your trail, he'd likely assume you'd gone on to Mexico, and it'd take him more time than it's worth to him to check and find you hadn't."

"And when I get to this San Bernardo place," Faro said, "I'll just look around and—what was it you called what you had to do?—start improvising, I guess."

"I expect you'll be good at it," Reid said. He smiled again, briefly, and Faro wondered just what it was the Ranger found so amusing.

He was not anticipating with any pleasure what he assumed would be his final interview with Rosa Schofield; but when he got back to his room, he found she had gone, along with her valise. The only traces of her presence were a hairpin on the pillow and a note on the bureau, which he read with interest and growing apprehension.

Dear Mr. Blake,
    The maid that came to make up the bed told me that Mr. Schofield had been asking around

and making a stir at the hotel. I think she guessed who I am, as you are only registered for a single room, and she might let on to him about where I was, so I am leaving here. If she doesn't, somebody else will. I had better try to find Mr. Schofield .before he finds me, as I have learned that I come out better if I can get the first word in.

I will try not to tell him who you are, but he is good at finding out what he wants to know, that being his business, so I think you had better move on while you can. I would not mind much if he caught Mr. Blanton, because he was not very good. Mr. Schofield is better than you, but you are pretty good.

Your well-wisher,
Rosa Schofield (Mrs.)

By noon, Faro had booked passage on the *Gulf Flyer,* reluctantly paying the full fare to Tampico in order to throw any later inquiries off the trail. The steamer was due to leave at three, and at this late hour, there was only deck passage available, at least for the first day or so. Luckily, the weather gave promise of staying clement.

At five past three, the ship's whistles and bells sounded and the gangplank was drawn in. Roustabouts cast off the lines that held it to the pier, and the *Gulf Flyer* began to edge into Galveston Harbor.

At six past three, a giant figure in a well-cut suit ran to the edge of the pier, unhesitatingly identified Faro at the rail—from Rosa's description? Faro wondered bitterly—and opened up his fusillade, sending Faro and his neighbor scrambling for shelter behind the cotton bales.

So, Faro reflected, his gabby fellow-passenger had the right of it: all the to-do *had* to come about through his winning a poker hand when he shouldn't have. . . .

He just hoped that Captain John Reid had been right about San Bernardo being a nice, quiet place to rest up in.

Chapter 3

Faro's opinion of Captain Reid's reliability as a travel agent plummeted sharply at his first view of what he took to be San Bernardo.

At Port Isabel he had debarked from the *Gulf Flyer* and taken passage on the *Harriet-Anne McCurdy,* a river steamer, enjoying the leisurely upstream trip. It tickled his fancy to think that he was spending days in, for all practical purposes, nowhere. Mexico was to his left, Texas to his right, and the river between them was truly a part of neither. For a man like himself, he thought in a rare philosophical moment, it was the right sort of place to be.

But now, with the end of his journey nearing, the boat's captain had informed him that they would be arriving at San Bernardo shortly before noon, and by eleven Faro was out on the river packet's deck with his valise and "tool case," anxious to debark. He would be the only passenger to do so. The tedious crawl up the Rio Grande had about sated his appetite for boat travel for some time, and he was anxious to get on shore.

Ahead, on the right—the American—side of the river, he saw a promontory covered with a straggle of low buildings, dominated by an irregular mass. As they drew closer, this resolved itself into a ruined stone building that had the look of a fort; and the buildings around it were a ragtag array of wood shacks and decaying adobe. The sounds Faro heard drifting from the place didn't accord with Reid's description of San Bernardo as a quiet backwater. Somebody seemed to be playing a concertina, not at all well. The wind bore an occasional shout or scream to him.

Still some distance off, he saw several figures at the river's edge. As he watched, two of these pursued a third along the bank. He heard the sound of a shot and saw the leading figure fall. The other two ran up to it, bent over it, then tipped it into the river.

What struck Faro most forcibly was that none of the others nearby—now close enough to be seen as roughly dressed men—made any attempt to stop the chase and murder, or even to take any particular interest in it.

He went quickly to the wheelhouse and approached the captain. "You got no objection, I believe I'll extend my passage a little farther upriver. What I've seen of San Bernardo so far, I doubt it's a place I'd care to visit. Frankly," he added, "I'm surprised you got the sand to put in there—the look of it, they'd be likely to burn you at the dock for fun."

"They would, and we ain't," the captain said. "San Bernardo's a way on yet. That there's Louse Point— *near* San Bernardo but not *of* San Bernardo, if you take my point. Fact, just what it's of`is hard to study out."

"Meaning?"

"Well, now it's to starboard, but time was when 'twas to port."

"Well, sure," Faro said. "Depends on which way you're headed. Downriver, it'll be on your left, or port, or hayfoot or whatever."

"That's so plain that I don't see why in thunder you said it," the captain said testily. "The facts of it is some different, an' worth listenin' to without ill-considered remarks."

As he explained it, Louse Point had until a few years ago been an unremarkable piece of Mexican riverfront property, distinguished only by its utter worthlessness. Once a minor military outpost, it had been abandoned after the Mexican War, and sheltered only a few nomadic outcasts. Then the usually placid but always tricky Rio Grande had cut a new channel and abandoned the old one, neatly transferring Punto Luis to the American side of the river.

"Thing is," the captain said, "that land's been Mex since there was a Mexico, not that they had much use for it lately. An' now here it is, tied up fast to Texas, with no documents or treaties argued an' wrote out about it. Was only the hand of God that arranged the transfer, an' He don't cut much ice in Mexico City nor Washington, seems like."

The result was that Louse Point didn't belong properly to either nation. For Mexico to enforce its jurisdiction would have involved crossing a recognized international border, the river. For the U.S. to do so would have meant claiming territory long possessed by Mexico and never relinquished. Eventually it would doubtless be sorted out—the bureaucrats on both sides privately prayed for another prank by the Rio Grande, preferably one which would wash away Louse Point entirely. But meanwhile the promontory existed in an international vacuum that was quickly filled by a number of minor outlaws and crooks who had figured out that they would be safe from harassment by either Mexican or U.S. authorities. And their calculations had proved correct: *rurales, federales,* U.S. Marshals, and Texas Rangers were alike barred from pursuing any known or suspected felons into Louse Point. It was never agreed on whether the area had acquired its name by corruption of its original Mexican title or as a description of the new residents.

"So it just lays there festerin' in the sun," the captain concluded, "breedin' all kinds of wickedness an' corruption. My personal opinion, that place is overdue for a dose of fire an' brimstone, though a good plague might do the job at less cost per head."

"It's a relief to find out that ain't San Bernardo," Faro said.

The captain shook his head. "Quiet a place as a man'd want to find, neat an' orderly, an' prosperin' now that Alex McGree has started drivin' trail herds up to Kansas. He runs his ranch the way a ranch should be run, an' Mal Holabird pretty well runs the town as well as the main store an' bank. Last time I was up, end of winter, I had to lay over a day or so for repairs, an' I never see a place so pleasant an' peaceful."

With a nightmare feeling of reliving a situation he hadn't liked a hell of a lot the first time, Faro dove behind a pile of cotton bales next to a storage shed by the San Bernardo pier, with the angry whine of a bullet in his ears.

From the sound of it, he wasn't the target this time, but there was no sense in courting accidents.

He winced as an answering shot came from somewhere to his left, and far closer than he would have liked, and cursed the impulse to chat with the captain that had kept him hanging around the pier until the *McCurdy*'s departure. But for that he'd have been well into San Bernardo by now, sampling whatever peace and quiet it had to offer, though by the present sample it might not be top quality.

Faro chanced a quick look from behind the sheltering bales. He could see the barrel of a rifle protruding from behind a cottonwood. Beyond it he could see the hundred yards of packed-earth street that led to the hub, such as it was, of San Bernardo: a two-story building that had the look of a bank, flanked by a few stores and an unmistakable saloon ranged along a plankwalk.

A movement to his left caught his eyes, and he swiveled to see a figure crouched behind a barricade of squat kegs. If they contained what he thought they did, there was another horrible resemblance to the situation he had experienced while departing from Galveston. . . .

The crouching man rose above the keg tops, triggered his revolver twice in the direction of the cottonwood, and settled back into his crouch.

The rifle boomed twice. Its second report was drowned in a succession of deep blasts that shook the ground and toppled a cotton bale onto Faro.

When he had wriggled out from under it, he looked toward the cottonwood and saw the rifleman vanish into the brush. The stench of burnt powder drifted to him, and he looked toward where the other gunman had been. There was a charred area on the ground, with burning wisps of grass, where the kegs had been. Above it hung a cloud of dark smoke, dissipating slowly. Faro saw at the far edge of it something that might have been a grotesquely shaped log about two yards long—but pretty certainly wasn't—which lay smoldering and blackened.

"Hey!" Faro turned to see a man jogging down the street that led from the town, "what's going on here?"

"Two fellows was taking shots at each other. One of 'em considered it was a sound plan to hide behind a couple kegs of blasting powder. Wasn't," Faro answered.

"Oh, Lord." The arrival, a plump man with a six-pointed star affixed to his vest, laid a hand indecisively on the six-shooter holstered at his waist.

He walked, every line of his body expressing distaste, toward the gnarled lump of charcoal that lay near where the powder kegs had been. "Which was he and which are you?" he asked Faro.

"Which out of what?" Faro said. "Don't you mean *who*? As for the unfortunate here—" They were now looking at the distorted form. "—there is enough left from the chest upwards so he don't seem to have had a beard, so it prob'ly ain't President Hayes. Beyond that, the way the blast took him, I'd say it's anybody's guess. I personally am Faro Blake, offloaded from the *Harriet-Anne McCurdy* not half an hour gone, and dropped into what I don't have any clear notion of."

"I meant," said the plump man, "are you McGree or Holabird, and do you know was that there one or the other whilst he was among us?"

Well, Faro thought, a man's brain don't have to click over like a Babbage adding machine to compute what's going on here. So fucking much for pleasant

36

and peaceful, I been set down in the middle of a feud!

"Now that is what is called a sleeve holdout," Faro said. "That clamp part is affixed to the scoundrel's forearm, which when he flexes it brings the card clamped into the claw on the front part right into the palm of his hand. And those there are shiner rings, which the man skilled in the ways of cheating can use like as a mirror to read the down sides of cards as they are being dealt out."

The star-toting plump man, now known to Faro as Town Marshal Enoch Pratt, pawed through the contents of Faro's tool case, opened on a table in the rear part of the Catamount Saloon, to which he had conveyed Faro after the recent explosive shootout.

"And this?" The marshal held up a soiled length of linsey-woolsey.

"A belly-band, for protection against the chill winds, set aside for laundering for when it'd be next required," Faro said blandly, hoping that the marshal's nostrils were not sensitive enough to detect the reek of gun oil that clung to it. Reasonably pleading a need, he had stepped aside at the first privy they had come to and, with the door closed, transferred the cutdown shotgun to the sling built into his coat, taking a chance on leaving its wrappings behind.

Pratt squinted at him shrewdly over the rim of his mug of beer, ordered at Faro's expense—a circumstance which seemed to indicate that Pratt was prepared to be reasonable. You don't work a nickle graft on a man if you're meaning to come down on him with the full force and majesty of the law.

"And you are telling me," Pratt went on, "that you travel about with them devices and contraptions, plus the marked cards and so, in order to explain to the impressionable youth how unscrupulous gamblers and sharps operate to fleece 'em of their hard-earned coin?"

"Well, yes." It wasn't much of a story, but once it had become clear that Pratt meant to interview him and go over his belongings, Faro'd had to come up with something.

"It's my belief you're no lecturer, but a gambling man, and these is your cheating tools," Pratt said, puncturing Faro's hopes of having created a plausible deception.

"One way of putting it," Faro said cautiously, taking a pull at his beer.

"Good," Pratt said heavily.

"Not the usual line of talk from a marshal under the circumstances," Faro ventured.

Pratt rolled his eyes upward. "Three months back or so, I'd have had you in the *calabozo* quick as winking, with all your stuff confiscated and broke up, fined you for what funds you had on you, and booted you out of town. But the way things are now, you're small potatoes, and I don't need you on my plate. Was a pickpocket to come into San Bernardo now, I'd greet him as a man and brother, and direct him to where his fingers could best do their work. That's how low law enforcement has sunk in San Bernardo."

"I am sorry to hear it," Faro said. "Aside from the business about me being jailed, looted and booted, which I will take as being meant to add color and force to your story. How does it come about that you'd rather I was the low-down type of gambler you seem to take me for than something else?"

"Because if you're a gambler, a snake-oil merchant or an electric-belt salesman, or anything in the line of peaceable larceny, the odds are you ain't some hired gun brought in by the McGrees or the Holabirds," Pratt said bitterly.

"The feud has got to that kind of doings, then?" Faro asked, motioning to the bartender to fetch over another brace of beers.

"If you just got here, where'd you hear about the feud?" Pratt said suspiciously.

"The fireworks down there, and your questions about the McGrees and the Holabirds, gave me the idea that something like that was going on," Faro said. "All I knew before I got here was that a Holabird sees to it that the town ticks over the way it ought to, and that a McGree trims the fat off of the land in the shape of cattle. I got to take it, though, that this arrangement has come untied lately, and they have taken to disagreeing with some violence?"

"Yah," Pratt said. "There was a little trouble between 'em, I heard, a long time back, so they ain't been friends much since I been here, but they always worked well together in a business way when they had to. But the last couple of months, that's all fallen apart. There's been barns burned and robberies done and cattle run off and men killed and so on. Each thing that happens makes it harder to get the whole shitpoke of it cleared up." He took a pull at his beer mug.

"Well, I don't see that you could go at 'em like a Sunday school teacher and tell 'em to shake hands and make up like little gentlemen," Faro said. "But when it comes to felonies and misdemeanors and promiscuous explosions, would seem to me that you, being the law hereabouts, would be doing something about that."

"What with?" Pratt asked bitterly. "Way things

used to be, was there some trouble, I would get the loan of a few fellows from Holabird's warehouse or McGree's ranch, and it'd be took care of in no time. But now it's them, or those that's siding them, that's breaking the law, and there ain't much of anything I can do about it except pick up the pieces. And it's looking to get worse."

"You mean bringing in outside gunslingers?" Faro asked.

The marshal nodded. "There's been men showing up lately that I don't know nor like the look of, nor can't get straight answers from—and they ain't the sort you can question too closely. Some I think are from Louse Point—you know about that?—and the others could be from anywhere. When one side or the other feels they got enough firepower, it's my feeling they'll start another Bull Run here."

"I can see you'd find that more 'n you'd want to handle on your own," Faro said.

"*Want* don't come into it," Pratt replied. "It's the plain fact that I *can't*. I got to have help on this, and I've asked for it, though God knows when it'll get here."

Before Faro could ask what kind of help the marshal had in mind, Pratt leaned toward him and whispered, "There's one of 'em now," as he gestured at a tall man entering the Catamount, dressed in range gear of a dark hue. Faro missed seeing his face, as he was mopping it with a bandana as he passed them on the way to the bar.

"One of them that's drifted in lately. Whether the McGrees or the Holabirds brung him in, I've no more way of finding out than the babe unborn, but he's got the look of a man that knows to handle a gun. Ain't done nothing, and turns any questions away polite, so

I got no cause to arrest him, but he smells like danger to me."

Faro squinted at the tall man, who now stood at the bar, facing away from the table where he and the marshal sat. He did look dangerous, sure enough. His bearing also seemed oddly familiar. Faro ran over in his mind the catalogue of itinerant gunmen he was acquainted with, and found himself unable to assign this man a place in it.

"I can see you got yourself a pailful of tarantulas to deal with here, Marshal," he said. "One thing I'd admire to know, though, as it damn near got me killed —what the hell is this feud all about?"

Chapter 4

"For the fulness of it," Pratt said, "you got to go back thirty years an' more, to the fight with Mexico—the second one, that is."

Mal Holabird and Alex McGree, young immigrants and then fervent "Texians," had fought Santa Anna's forces to achieve independence from Mexico in 1836, and in the aftermath of their victory had prospered, one as a rancher, the other as a banker and tradesman. Nine years later, Texan, Mexican, and American politics threw them into another conflict with the same adversary. McGree and Holabird, older now, were inclined to sit on what they had and hope for the best, and San Bernardo might have remained a backwater during the struggle had it not been for the appearance of one Robert Locksley on the scene early in the year of 1846.

Locksley, an energetic, persuasive and well-traveled

young man, convinced McGree and Holabird that it was unmanly—and worse, boring—to fight a purely defensive war. They could do something interesting about the fort at Punto Luis. To capture it and raise the Stars and Stripes from its ramparts might strike such dismay into Santa Anna's heart that he would drop any plans for invading San Bernardo—a worthwhile tactical victory. Or it might provoke him to launch an attack in force, which could make for a hell of a lot of fun for men with a taste for powder smoke.

Given the go-ahead by Holabird and McGree— even as young men the leading voices in the area— Locksley had scouted into Mexico to spy out the fort's defenses. A plausible talker with a good command of Spanish, he passed himself off as a loyal subject of the Mexican government to the garrison, and accomplished his mission, returning with a bonus piece of news. A paymaster and military escort were expected in a few days, bringing long-overdue back pay to the Border garrisons. Thus, if the campaign were handled right, the Texan force could not only strike a blow at the enemy, but come out considerably the richer for their effort.

Locksley worked out the strategy; and, following his plan, Holabird and McGree and about a dozen of their followers rafted across the river near midnight. A drowsy sentry was easily overwhelmed and the fort taken with only token resistance. The garrison was herded off to captivity by half the Texans; the remainder occupied the fort and waited for the pay party.

This duly arrived, and was welcomed with blasts from the fort's ordnance. Locksley, acting as master cannoner, directed the fire to disable the paymaster's wagon and drive off the escort. As planned, he, Mc-

Gree and Holabird rode out to retrieve Santa Anna's gold from the wrecked vehicle.

At this point the plan ran somewhat off its track. Locksley had not allowed for the chance of the Mexican escort counterattacking, which it did. McGree and Locksley managed to carry the heavy chest containing the gold with them as they retreated and fired. Under cover of night, they slipped out of the fort and gained the river bank where their boats were moored; but before they were across the Rio Grande, the Mexican troops had come up to them and brought them under heavy fire. One boat was holed and sunk, but most of its occupants reached the far shore. When the fleeing Texans counted noses back in San Bernardo, they were shy only one man, Locksley. They were also shy one chest, thought to contain upwards of fifty thousand dollars in gold pesos. McGree and Holabird agreed that the chest must have gone down in the sunken boat, and also agreed to mourn the gallant Locksley, gone bravely to a soldier's—or, to be accurate, a sailor's—grave.

"That was about the last they truly agreed, though," Pratt said. "For 'twas about that time that McGree come into some money from a relative back east, and was able to build up his herds pretty considerable. And Holabird done well in some speculations out in California, which brought him in enough so's he could set up his bank. Now, there was nothing open said about it, but there was them that wondered if McGree's relative back east had ever really been, and that he might of hid the chest of gold after the fight and been drawing on it. And it seemed to some it could be that Holabird's money might of come originally from Mexico, not California. Wasn't ever anything public about it, like I said, but it must of got to them, some ways, because they was never really friends after. McGree needed Holabird's bank and stores, and Holabird needed the money and trade McGree's ranching brought in, and they both needed things to keep running orderly, so they worked together, but one of 'em or both had worked up a kind of smidgen of mistrust of the other."

This relationship had in the last few months deteriorated disastrously.

"Some McGree cousin, Jim by name, drifted in from over to Arkansas, where he'd been a farmhand; and, about that time, Bob Holabird, Mal's youngest, that run off when a tad owing to a knife scrape he got into whilst boozed up, come back looking for the prodigal son treatment. He didn't get any fatted calf, but Mal had a place set for him at the supper table and give him a job in the general store. Firstest thing you know, Jim McGree and Bob Holabird was eyeing each other like roosters at a cockfight—blood enemies on sight, it looked like. And Bob would bad-mouth Jim to any that'd listen, and throw in the rest of the McGrees for good measure; and Jim would set it about that Bob was low enough to walk under a snake without taking his hat off, which was only to be expected, seeing as he was a Holabird. And both of 'em brought up the old business about the Mex gold. Then some McGree cattle got run off, and it was taken as Gospel that the Holabirds done it; and the warehouse was cleaned out of a lot of stuff, and hardly a townsman don't lay that to McGree's account. My own thought is that it could be some of them from Louse Point that's into it. Any road, it's now a settled thing that McGrees and Holabirds is sworn enemies, and there's markers out in the cemetery to prove it. I don't know how to tot up this last one that got blowed up, as he ain't got much about him left for putting a name to."

"Could be one of the drifters you was talking about," Faro said. "Like the one that come in here a while back. You might could ask him if he's got a pal that's turned up missing."

"Maybe," the marshal said dubiously. "Here he comes now. Yo, Blanton!" Faro spluttered on his beer at the name, and looked up at the tall man who had paused by the table.

It was not Rosa's temporary proprietor, but Faro knew very well why he had thought that there was something familiar about him. He also had a strong suspicion about how his own presence in San Bernardo had been brought about.

"Marshal?" the tall man said, ignoring Faro.

"Would like a word with you," Pratt said.

The tall man said, "You've been curious about me and my business since I got here, and maybe the time's come to deal with that. But not here, I'd say. If you're in your office in about ten minutes, I believe I'll drop by and we can talk in privacy. Bring this gentleman with you if you want."

He nodded to Pratt and Faro, and left the saloon.

"What do you make of that?" Pratt marveled.

Faro finished his beer and said, "Hardly worth brooding on, as that . . . Blanton says he's about to lay it out for you in a while."

"Wonder why he mentioned special that you could come along?" the marshal persisted.

"Them traveling gunmen is given to fancies that law-abiding gamblers and marshals don't entertain," Faro said sourly. "There is no figuring them. I would say we'd best humor him on the point. I will listen with interest to what he has to say."

Especially, he told himself, what the son-of-a-bitch has to say about shipping me up here so as to get away from the unwelcome attentions of Ben Schofield in peaceful and boring surroundings!

Chapter 5

"Well hey," Pratt said plaintively, handing back the star and the much-creased commission that identified "Blanton" as Captain John Reid, Texas Rangers, "I don't want to seem picky about this, but I wired off to Austin for emergency help, and I don't know what good I'm going to get out of one lone Ranger."

"You've only got one lone feud," Reid said. He tilted back in his chair and surveyed the marshal's office, the marshal, and Faro with a level stare.

"I had more in mind something on the lines of a company, and a battalion wouldn't be overmuch to deal with what's coming, as I see it," Pratt complained.

"A big bunch of men is fine if you're working up a war," Reid said, "but if you had your battalion or company of Rangers, there's not a thing they could do but shoot up half your citizens to protect the other half. So it's Adjutant General Steel's decision that

I'm to handle it—with the assistance of my colleague, Mr. Blake, here."

Faro squinted at Reid, but kept his peace. Colleague, my ass, he told himself.

"Thisyer's another Ranger?" Pratt asked.

"Not a Ranger, but a special operative," Reid assured him. "Mr. Blake is versed in the ways of the devious and low class of men that seem to be involved in your troubles here."

"She and it," Pratt said. "I got to take it that you're what you say you are, and he's what you say he is. But I will tell you, the taking of them propositions don't mean for a instant that I got any hope that you'll bring about what you're talking of. It seems to me that it'll take a sight more than a Ranger operative and a Ranger captain to better the situation."

"Stranger things have happened," Reid said.

"For sure, but not outside of Scripture, as it seems to me you're talkin' about passin' a miracle or so. And my experience has led me to conclude that West Texas ain't one of the places the Almighty is overmuch concerned with."

"He may or may not be," Reid said, "but General Steele is. The General's sent me here, along with Mr. Blake, to work all this out. We will of course do this with your full help and cooperation, and the first instalment of that is that your lips are sealed about who we are and what we're here for."

"I guess," Pratt said gloomily. "Was me that sent off to Ranger headquarters in Austin about all this in the first place. I am as against arsons and shootings and batteries and torts and explosions, as any man that draws breath. But you got to understand how I'm sited here."

"I do," Reid said. "You are pretty well a chore boy for McGree and Holabird, and your bosses have fallen out, and I'm here to carry the can for you. Now, you will be happy to allow us some private time for discussing these matters," Reid said, settling back into the chair he occupied.

"It will certainly be my pleasure to leave you two gents here and take myself elsewheres, I'll allow you that," Pratt said drily.

As the marshal closed the door of his office behind him, Faro fetched out his hammered silver flask and asked Reid, "Care for a snort?"

The Ranger captain shook his head. "Not on the job. I need my wits clear for what has to be done. In fact, I think even the off-duty social imbibement of strong drink may be getting to me. There have been nighttime ranklings I don't like, and feelings about the tongue and temples in the mornings that are out-and-out alarming. It may be that I have got a constitution that ardent spirits are poison to, and have inflicted damage to it. Before leaving Galveston, I was fortunate to run across a medical sort of practitioner who allowed me to buy from him a few bottles of his specific against just that kind of ailment, and I have to say that it's done wonders for me."

He fetched a flat, dark-green bottle from his pocket and displayed it to Faro, who squinted and inspected the label. "Sachem Onondaga's Curative Bitters and Tonic," he read. "Sounds impressive."

"It is," Reid said. "Any ranklings come on, and the Bitters and Tonic quiets them in no time." He pulled the stopper from the bottle and took a gulp. "Feel its benefits already," he declared.

Faro imagined that he probably did. Most of these

51

remedies, as outlined to him once by Doc Prentiss, consisted of something like a quarter grain alcohol, some herb flavoring, and a substantial dose of opium. "I believe I will make do with my own tonic," he said, and tossed down a capful of bourbon from his flask. "Now, getting to this colleague stuff, I got to tell you it's not in the cards."

"Ah, but it is," Reid said. "I dealt them and that's how they fall. I conned you into coming out here, as you'll have already deduced, and I aim to use you. Not an hour after I got that telegram from General Steele putting me onto this job, there you were with your problem with Ben Schofield, so I improvised you onto the scene where you could be some help. You traveling by boat gave me time to get on over here some faster by stage and spy out the situation in San Bernardo ahead of time so's I could work you into my plans."

"Well, work me out of 'em," Faro said. "You got me here, but you can't keep me."

"No," the Ranger said, "I can't. At least, not without damaging you some, like breaking your kneecaps, which would cut down on your usefulness. No," Reid mused, "that doesn't seem to fit in right now. So, like you say, you could leave. But remorse would follow you the rest of your days when you thought on how you'd had the chance to help preserve the peace of Texas and run off from it."

"I believe I could manage to forget that in time," Faro said uneasily.

"No, there would be reminders." Reid shook his head sadly.

"What kind of reminders?" Faro wanted to know.

Reid shrugged. "It's not for me to say how a man's

conscience operates to make him regret failing in his duty. It could come about in any number of ways. For instance, a mention in General Steele's directory."

Faro wondered if the Sachem's tonic contained more than the usual ration of opium. "What's a directory got to do with it?"

"General Steele has labored long to compile a list of close to three thousand bad men shaming Texas by their presence," Reid said. "This is kept at and consulted by every Ranger post, and every Ranger officer studies it over carefully, so's he can recognize and deal with any man that's listed therein. Now, no system is perfect, and it might be that some name got added that didn't belong—say by some telegram sent in from the field and not rightly understood—and it could be a long time, if ever, before that name got taken off that list. Especially," he added, "if it was noted that the man was known to be armed, dangerous, and determined not to be taken alive. Now, that could be the kind of reminder I mean."

"Would certainly refresh a man's memory powerfully if he happened to be anywhere in Texas," Faro said, mentally deleting Galveston, San Antonio, and Austin from his future ports of call.

"General Steele's directory is borrowed, consulted, and regarded as gospel in all states and territories," Reid said. "Copies have also gone to Canada and the Sandwich Islands."

"Well, now." Faro considered his situation. On the one hand, he could get himself planted on General Steele's shit list, with the kind of biography that would be a standing invitation to any lawman in the English-speaking world to shoot him on sight. On the other, he could accept the fact that this hophead Ranger had

dealt from the bottom, cooperate with him, and maybe
build up some credit with the authorities that could be
drawn on in some tight spot or other in the future.

He was on what Doc Prentiss used to call the horns
of a dilemma, but Reid had made it clear that one
horn was razor-sharp and ready to be pushed all the
way up his ass.

"I got to thank you," Faro said, "for recalling my
duty as a citizen to me in them eloquent terms. Captain Reid, I am your man."

What Reid required of Faro, it developed, was that
he insinuate himself into the McGree faction's stronghold, old Alex's ranch, and gain the patriarch's trust.
"I have seen enough feuds hereabouts to know how
they usually go," he said, "and this one has a kind of
wrong smell to it. There's things that don't fit the way
they should, and I've got to know just what's going on
before I can decide how best to stop it. It'll be up to
you to find that out from the McGree side."

"I don't know as I'd be much at home on a ranch,"
Faro said. "I am more the town type. Why don't you
let me sniff around the Holabirds here in town?"

Reid shook his head. "McGree's men have spotted
me drifting around their land, seeing what I could
make out without getting too close, and I'd say they've
got it into their heads that I was spying on them for
the Holabirds. Be a job to get them to trust me."

"Nor they wouldn't me any easier, I'd say," Faro
argued.

Reid countered with the suggestion that Faro pass
himself off as a distant McGree cousin, just arrived in
San Bernardo. He had looked into the family background and discovered two suitably distant branches,

the Jenkinses of South Carolina and the Bottomleys of Virginia—

"I'll settle for Jenkins," Faro said firmly. "I will hazard what I got to for the peace and safety of Texas, but not to the extent of parading myself as a Bottomley."

—and saw no difficulty in Faro's claiming the hospitality of his supposed relatives. Though tension was mounting daily, there was still some traffic between the ranch and the town and Faro should be able to contrive a means of communicating anything important he learned to Reid.

Marshal Pratt poked his head around the doorframe and said, "You gentlemen finished with my office yet? Chore boy I may be, but there is chores to be done, and this is where I see to them."

The marshal's sourness abated a little when Reid declared that his cooperation and help was vital to the plan, and disclosed his proposed stratagem. "Could work," he said thoughtfully. "Blake here—Jenkins, I mean," he amended at Reid's warning frown—"hasn't been around here long enough to get pegged as being with one side or the other, for one thing. And the time's right for it. When I was out just now I saw Alex's granddaughter, Dora McGree. Told me she'd come into town to pick up some dress goods Alex had ordered special for her. Her grandpa is set on her dressing ladylike, so she was obliged to have one of the hands drive her—"

"Leaving the lady's clothes out of it," Reid interrupted, "do I take it she's still about?"

"Should be," Pratt said. "Likely still in the drygoods store. You can tell that by whether there's a buckboard hitched outside."

"Then come on," Reid said to Faro, rising and striding from the marshal's office. Faro gathered his valise and case and followed as Reid turned into a short alleyway that led to San Bernardo's main street.

"Hey, wait," Faro said. "Where at are we rushing to?"

"You heard Pratt. Dora McGree's right here, your chance to meet her and get invited to the ranch."

"Well, now," Faro said uneasily. "I haven't studied out how I'm to do that. I think I'd better get it more settled in my mind, so the performance comes off easy and convincing."

Reid poked his head around a corner, and Faro, looking over his shoulder, saw a slim girl standing next to a hitched-up buckboard with a wiry man in the driver's seat holding the reins. She was holding a paper-wrapped parcel and talking with an apron-clad man at the door of a store.

"No time for that," Reid said. "She's about to leave. We'll have to improvise."

Reid grabbed Faro by the shoulders and gave him a shove that sent him stumbling into the street.

Hampered by the case and valise in either hand, he barely managed to regain balance; then Reid was coming at him, face contorted, and bawling hoarsely, "No goddam McGree c'n talk to me like that an' git away with it!"

"Hey—" Faro's head snapped back as a looping punch caught him on the cheekbone. He dropped the valise and case and brought his fists up.

Reid slammed him with a blow that jarred Faro's hat loose and seemed for a moment to have done the same for his head.

"And you can tell that old horned toad Alex Mc-

56

Gree that I'll do th' same fer anyone of his tribe that jumps salty with me!" Reid yelled, with a final kidney punch that sent Faro reeling into the dust of the street.

Through pain-dimmed eyes he watched the Ranger retreat to the alleyway and vanish as the girl ran up to him.

She was dressed for ranch life rather than the town in a buckskin skirt and gingham shirt, cut large. As she bent over him, he got an excellent, if brief, view of her breasts. Not as sumptuous as Rosa's, but nicely shaped all the same. If I had my breath and strength, I'd be enjoying that, he thought.

"Are you hurt?" she cried.

"Some," he wheezed.

"Why was that man hitting you?"

Struck by a fit of improvisation, Faro said bitterly but silently, "Hard to say. I was asking around after some kinfolk I have here, that I was thinking to look up, name of McGree, and he came over all contumacious and combative, and the next I knowed, I was sitting here in the road."

"Looked to me like the feller that some of us spotted riding around the spread some days back, Miss Dora," the wiry buckboard driver said, coming up to them. "Was in our minds, he was a Holabird man of some sort."

"I don't hold with that foolishness, Jed," the girl said. "Grandpa and Mal Holabird were friends for years, and it doesn't make sense that they're enemies now. He's seeing Holabirds under the bed, and so are all you hands."

Jed ignored this and squinted at Faro. "I heard him yelling before he decked you," he said. "About the

57

McGrees. I know all the McGrees, and you ain't one."

"Nor I ain't," Faro said. "As I was telling Miss Dora here, I am kin to them, name of Jenkins . . . uh, Sam Jenkins . . . from—"

"North Carolina!" Dora said, clapping her hands delightedly.

"Well, yes," Faro said, eyeing her open collar closely. She was still bent forward and the motion of her hands had set up a reciprocal tremor under her shirt that made him realize he was recovering from Reid's punishment faster than he had thought. "How does it come about that you'd know that?"

"I'm Dora McGree," the girl said. "Alex McGree's granddaughter—so I know all about our Jenkins cousins back east . . . and to think you're one of them! Isn't it just amazing that we'd meet this way?"

"I don't know when I been more taken by surprise," Faro said, honestly enough.

"Well, now," Dora went on, motioning to Jed to help her get Faro to his feet, "you'll have to come on out to our ranch—Grandpa will want to see you, and anyhow we could put you up more comfortably than you'd find in town. You will come, won't you?"

"I would admire to," Faro said. "If it wouldn't be trouble?"

"Trouble?" Jed said. "For McGree kin that has bled in the McGree cause—" Faro, rubbing his hand over his smarting nose and observing a crimson smear on his fingers "—there's no such thing as trouble!"

As Dora and Jed helped him onto the buckboard, Faro reflected that Reid's improvisation had been as effective as the Ranger could have wished—it had established Faro Blake as Cousin Sam Jenkins, and

58

doubtless given Reid himself some standing with the Holabird faction.

But if he's got any more improvisations as good as that one, Faro thought, easing himself onto the buckboard's padded rear seat alongside Dora, I hope he don't try them on me. I suspect another one as good as that would use me up entirely.

Chapter 6

"Well, hey," Alex McGree crowed. "I guess my three ladies got it over your jacks and kings, don't they?"

Faro laid down the just-losing hand he had dealt himself, watched his host gleefully rake in the pot, and sighed. "I would of bet a pretty that you'd have folded with that hand. I stood pat with two pair, which ain't the best odds, figuring I could bluff you."

McGree regarded Faro over the tops of his half-spectacles and sent his wispy beard jutting in a grin. "Nary a man around can truthfully say he's bluffed Alex McGree, Sam," he said. "Alex McGree takes the cards he is dealt and plays them, and usually manages to win, especially when it counts. You get the cards you was meant to get—play 'em as you see 'em, and you won't go far wrong."

"Well, now," Faro said, sliding the cards together and shoving them over toward McGree for the next deal, "it would seem to me that you've done pretty well following that rule, this spread and all."

He had certainly been impressed, earlier that afternoon, by what he'd seen of the Lazy M: the rambling two-story ranch house and outbuildings, corrals and stock pens; and, as Dora had proudly proclaimed, grazing land reaching as far as the eye could see.

Old Alex had welcomed him warmly as kin, doubly so as a man who had suffered in the McGree cause, and installed him in a spacious bedroom in the ranch house as an honored guest. At a welcomely lavish supper, he had met McGree's—and, for the moment, his—distant cousin Jim, a stocky, whiskered man in his twenties with a piney-woods twang to his speech that marked him as originating in Arkansas.

After the meal, Dora had retired to her room, and Jim had gone off to socialize with the hands in the bunkhouse—"Does them good, Uncle Alex," he had said, "to see that the family's working men like they are."

Faro had reserved judgment on the genial, talkative Jim, who had to be a key figure in the McGree-Holabird equation. Dora had been enchantingly demure in a conventionally feminine dinner frock. Old Alex had struck him as a piece of whang-leather—tough enough to crack teeth on.

"Still playing the hand I was dealt forty years and more back," Alex McGree said. "Came out here in '35, soft-talked by the Mex government, that wanted colonists then, to be a buffer 'twixt them and the Apaches, and took up this land. And I've held on to it through the times we got independent, and the war when we joined the Union, and the war when we tried to unjoin it, in '61. And I will say I've made it prosper, when other men has gone under and given up. Now all that has took a long time, Sam Jenkins, and I will tell you something about long times." McGree stared at the cards ranged before him, gathered them together and set them in their case.

"Now, a Texian that has the recollection of the Alamo clear in his mind as if it was yesterday, and came away from Goliad, like me, you'd say that there's a man who'd slit the throat of Santa Anna, any time, any place, given the chance."

McGree sighed and flicked a glance at Faro. "A few years back, I done well enough by getting my herd up to Dodge City before some of the other fellows so that I could give myself a holiday, the which I took in the fleshpots of Chicago. And there I run acrost an old man—*another* old man, I'll be honest about that—from down around these parts. Now, this old man had been up, and now he was down. In fact, he was sunk so low he was trying to sell some businessman there, name of Wrigley, some fool idea of selling people tree sap to chew on instead of tobacco, that's how far he'd come down from what he'd been. And him and me, we talked over the old times and the wars, as you'd expect when old men meet, that has been through the same things. Only that was Santa Anna. And all that hate I had for him, from '36 on, that didn't count for spit when I sat across a table from him and saw him old and shaky."

McGree gave Faro a somber look. "So I learned then that hate don't last as long as you think it might. And that is a good thing for a man to learn in the evening of his days. What ain't so good is to learn that other things don't last either." He fell silent, staring at the table.

"You and Mal Holabird," Faro ventured.

"Yah," McGree said after a long pause. "We was friends for years, even through the War, when I held with the Confederacy and he didn't. Mal and me, we whipsawed this country together and made it pay out, him in the trading and me in the ranching. And we mounted a damn good fight together, along with that poor Locksley fellow, against the Mexes in '45. And now we are both pretty near the end of our strings, and, God knows why, he's turned against me."

Undressing later in his room, Faro pondered on the old rancher's words. If he was telling the truth, the feud had not been of his seeking. So it had to be some unprompted malice on the part of Mal Holabird, which didn't make much sense, or . . . something else entirely.

"The money won't be as much," Jim McGree said, "but it'll be soon and on the nail."

Riding out with Faro to show him the extent of the McGree spread and to explain its operation, he had been filling his "cousin" in on the details of the upcoming trail drive. Unlike previous years, this was to be a short one—a few hundred miles to the east only.

"With this trouble with the Holabirds," Jim said, "we can't muster enough of a crew to go all the way to Kansas. We can haze them over to join up with some pal of Uncle Alex's, who'll take them over and pay off for them."

"I expect that'll be enough to meet the mortgage payments on the old homestead?" Faro hazarded.

"All the stock gets there, the agreed-on price is twenty thousand," Jim said. "Would fetch forty and up in Dodge, but we're spared the risk and the cost of trail hands for that long of a haul."

"You been on such a drive?" Faro asked.

"Not at any thirty dollars a month and found," Jim said. "For that kind of work, there is always fellows to be hired for the doing of it."

Faro eased himself on the saddle of his mount—in his view, a civilized man either walked, preferably on solid pavement, or rode in a well-sprung carriage, a parlor car or well-appointed ship, and not on top of a balky animal that should have been left off the Ark on the grounds of idiocy and inbred criminal tendencies —and looked at Jim with some interest.

"You got the ambition to live higher off the hog than the general run of West Texians?" he said.

"Well, now," Jim answered, "I am, come down to it, the next male McGree after Uncle Alex, what with his own boy, Dora's pa, dead these five years. The Lazy M has got to pass on to somebody that knows what to do with it."

"Hell," Faro said, wincing. His horse had just varied its plodding gait to prance around a chuckhole, and the unexpected bounce had come close to emasculating him.

"Well, he is me, stands to reason," Jim said, throwing Faro a sharp glance. "Uncle Alex is getting on, but he ain't so soft at the top that he'd turn the spread over to a woman, on the grounds that she's his nearest blood kin."

Faro raised himself slightly in the saddle and reached down and scrabbled his privates out of danger. "What you're saying is, when time gets all full up, you figure the Lazy M will come to you instead of Miss Dora?"

"She is closer kin," Jim said, "but it ain't in the nature of things that a woman should inherit property, especially any that is worth bothering about."

"If you have the right of that," Faro wanted to know, "what'd happen if Dora was to marry up with some fellow that'd have the savvy and the sand to play the man's part and hold the place for her?"

Ahead of them on a sandy rise a prairie dog stood up and surveyed their approach. Jim drew his revolver from the holster at his waist and squeezed off a shot. Dust fountained, the rodent gave a chittering scream and vanished into the sunbaked ground.

"Vermin," Jim said. "Hate the sight of 'em. Eating up a man's substance, and nothing to show for it. Now you was asking about Dora," he went on. "I will tell you, my true feeling and opinion is that Cousin Dora's main attraction is the name of McGree. She is a lady, though not enough refined to really make it in that line of work; but she ain't enough woman to draw in any fellows on her own account alone. Of tits and ass, she ain't carrying enough freight to give a man any kind of comfortable jouncing. And she got a way of talking and a way of looking at a man that low-rates him for fair, without nothing being said nor done in the open that you could take objection to. So I am not figuring that there will be any Mister Dora McGree coming along to clutter things up. Nor anybody else, that might have a notion to decide as he was entitled to some place in the old man's thoughts."

Faro reflected briefly on the fact that Jim's shot at the prairie dog, at something over a hundred yards, had come within an inch or so of it—and said carefully, "As a Jenkins from the Carolinas, I seen it as my due and my duty to pay a call to my distant connection here, Cousin Alex, and soak up some of his hospitality for a while. That is as far as it goes."

"Hey, we understand each other, Cousin Sam," Jim said. "I hope your stay with us here at the Lazy M will be pleasant and restful. Though with them Holabirds carrying on as they has been, there could be some excitements. It'll be good to have another reliable man on the spot in case they try anything. That Bob Holabird and the rest of his tribe of hydrophobia skunks is poison-mean enough to be up to all sorts of low doings, and a man can't hardly think of a trick awful enough that they wouldn't pull it."

"And that is the bunkhouse," Jim McGree said. "Next, we'll get on to where the branding's going on."

"If it is okay, cousin, I will pass on that," Faro said. "I am not in the ranching business nor hope to be, and now that I have seen where the cows hang around, and the chuckwagon, and the water holes, I would say that I have had what I need of the grand tour of the Lazy M. Why don't you go on, and I'll just sit around here for a while and do some restful talking."

"Please yourself," Jim said, evidently not much minding the prospect of missing out on Faro's company for the rest of his round of duty. "Now, you fellows," he went on, addressing the half-dozen cowhands in the bunkhouse, "I want you to keep a eye out for whatsoever as them Holabirds are up to. I want you to know that both Alex and me are relying on you to see that no Holabird does his dirty work on McGree stock or McGree land."

With a nod to Faro, he left the bunkhouse.

After a moment's silence, a rangy cowhand uncoiled himself from the bunk on which he had been lying and said mildly, "That was a man-sized portion of eloquence was just dropped onto us, for fair."

Another man stooped, picking up a shovel from in front of the empty coal stove that heated the frame building in winter, scraped it along the floor, and strode to the door. "It's all right now," he said, jerking the implement he held as if to empty it of a burden, "I have flang it out to ripen in the sun."

"Take it," Faro said, "that you fellows don't glory

67

in the prospect of fighting off the forces of evil as represented by the Holabirds?"

The senior hand present, a stocky man of close to forty, shrugged his shoulders. "When the War was on, I done my time in that, and it give me my fill of shooting and getting shot at. Also give me the notion that shooting and getting shot at is a piss-poor way for a man to spend his time. Most of the men here is too young to have gone through that, but neither them nor me has got much patience with such foolishness. It's no easy job to get a bunch of longhorns together and drive 'em to where they're supposed to be, and there's a mort of ways a man can get stove up or killed whilst at it. Stampedes, twisters, hailstorms, rattlesnakes, or just getting throwed by a horse and breaking your neck —them'll do me fine to watch out for, without getting feuds into it. If there is men with a dislike of Alex Mc-Gree that adds themselves into them hazards, I guess we will have to be ready to handle that, but I ain't about to figure I am enlisted in a noble cause. I done that once, which will satisfy me for the rest of my life."

The grim mood occasioned by the cowhand's comments was broken by the appearance through the bunkhouse doorway of a close-cropped head, from which came a guttural query: "Anybody for a haircut? Some of you fellers is getting so shaggy, Buffalo Bill'd shoot you on sight. In puttickler you, Shorty. A couple little horns, and wouldn't nobody question how your head'd look stuck up on a wall."

"I seen how you sheared some of the fellows," the stocky hand said, running his fingers through a curly mane of hair, "and I ain't anxious to be served so. But it ain't as restful as it used to be to go to the barber's in San Bernardo, what with all this feuding shit—so, okay, Owgooste, bring your clippers in and get at it."

The cropped head grinned and vanished.

"When I met that fellow at the chuckwagon when Jim was showing me around," Faro said to Shorty, "he was represented to me as the cook. He a barber that cooks for a pastime, or what?"

Shorty grinned. "You ain't never run acrost a trail cook before, I'd guess. We don't get to take our mamas on a drive with us, so somebody has got to see to them kinds of things that a mother'd do. Owgooste cuts hair, plus he does mending if someone's clothes get tore or a button comes off."

"Mends hide, too," another hand ventured. "I got a slash on my laig last year on the drive, an' Owgooste stitched 'er up an' rubbed some coal oil on to keep 'er from mortifyin'. It hurt worse'n any such stuff a doc ever used on me, so you c'n tell Owgooste knows his sawbonin'."

"No doubting of it," Shorty said, "you could do without any of the hands, at a pinch even the trail boss, if the men knows their jobs, but without a damn good cook, there just ain't no drive."

"I thought Jim was showing you around the ranch," Dora McGree said, meeting Faro in front of the ranch house after he had stabled his borrowed horse.

"He done that," Faro said. "Or at least as much of it as I was primed to take in all at once. I passed when he offered me the chance to sit in at the branding. If I am going to watch poker-work designs being burned onto leather, I'd as soon the leather ain't yelling out about it."

"Huh," she said, "it doesn't hurt 'em that much or that long. And since they're raised for slaughter, any-how, I don't see that it makes much odds. It's really

something to see a good branding crew at work—
they'll have a critter down, branded, and on its way
before it's started to bawl. And after that, all the way
to the stockyards, it's a Lazy M animal for all to see,
so there's no mistake about who gets paid for it."

Faro studied her with interest. Her blue-checked
gingham dress displayed her lithe figure agreeably,
and her fine-spun reddish hair was carefully and be-
comingly dressed. About the only thing that outwardly
distinguished her from the standard model of a well-
bred young woman was her sun-browned face and
hands, testifying to the absence of the customary sun-
bonnet and gloves. But her matter-of-fact attitude toward the basics of the ranching business marked her
even more surely as being something out of the ordi-
nary.

"You pay attention to all this stuff, then?" he said.

Dora nodded. "I'd better. It'll be mine some day,
and I don't propose to turn the Lazy M over to some
hired foreman. It'll be my inheritance and my responsibility, so I'll be seeing to the running of it. That re-
minds me, I was on the way to the barn. There's still
some of last year's hay in the loft, and I want to see
if it's still good. Do you want to walk over there with
me? There's no hot irons or yelling cattle about it,"
she added, with a slight grin that suggested she knew
how she had upset his preconception of her.

"Glad to," Faro said, and fell into step beside her.
"Might be a job, one woman running a spread like
this," he commented, thinking of Jim McGree's calm
assumption of succeeding to the Lazy M's ownership
or at the least effective control. "Could be you'd find it
easier if there was a . . . partner involved." He thought
that it might be worthwhile to sound Dora out on the

question of whether she might be considering any romantic entanglements that would upset Jim's plans.

She stopped suddenly and squinted at him. "You mean anything in particular by that?"

"No," he said, suddenly alert. He seemed to have hit on something that affected her strongly. "Was just that it seemed to me, a lone woman, it'd be . . ." He sketched a vague gesture in the air, realizing that it would not put him in any very good standing with Dora to suggest that she was incompetent to handle the fortunes of the Lazy M on her own. Girls in St. Louis or Chicago would glory in being incapable in men's business, but West Texas seemed to be different.

"Well, I could do it, no question," Dora said briskly. "But I will own that partnering has come to my mind. This silly feud, though, that's made some problems about that. A McGree and a Holabird joining up to run the Lazy M—the way things are going, that'd be a scandal that'd last up into the next century."

Now it was Faro who stopped in his tracks.

"For a stranger to San Bernardo, what though I'm a connection of your family," he said carefully, "I have heard substantial talkings concerning the McGrees and the Holabirds. But none of them touches on any present-day ties, links nor yokes. Are you telling me in some slaunchwise way that you and Bob Holabird . . . ?" He had pitched on the one Holabird he had heard of who was of an age reasonable to consider as a possible interest for Dora. If there were a Romeo-and-Juliet angle to the feud, it was something Reid ought to know about, and soon.

"I have known Bob Holabird since I wasn't much bigger than a jackrabbit," Dora said flatly. "One thing Bob Holabird used to do, he used to find some slough where toad-frogs and pollywogs were, and drop a flat

71

rock onto them, and laugh like a coyote. What he tried to get up to with me, I wouldn't care to say. In fact, I never did say it, or else this feud business would have started long ago—Grandpa would have gelded Bob, then butchered him and salted him down for the winter."

"Then it's some other Holabird you're studying up to marry?" Faro asked.

Dora passed before him into the shade of the barn, and gave him a sharply amused look. "No," she said, "the laws and my inclination don't run that way. Stella's don't, either."

"Stella?" Faro asked. His voice, echoing in the empty barn where they now stood, sounded hollowly foolish to him.

"Bob's sister, a few years younger than him, and my best friend," Dora said. "Ever since my pa died, and I knew I was to come into the Lazy M some day, we have had it fixed between us that she and I would run it. She'd have money from Mal—either by inheriting it or by gift, as she's his favorite—and with that and what I'll have picked up by seeing how things are done, we could make a real go of it, build it up to a lot bigger than what Grandpa's been able to. If he and Mal Holabird had been willing to throw in, years past, this could have been about the biggest ranch in Texas, but there's never been enough money to do that. When it's Stella's and my turn, well, things'll be different."

"Wouldn't your husband, when as you take one on, opine that it was his job to be seeing to them things?" Faro asked.

Dora shrugged and leaned against the ladder that led to the hayloft. "The few that's come courting seem to have had ideas that way. There we'd be on the front porch of an evening, with the fellow maybe

worked up enough to hold my hand, and he'd be looking out across what he could see of the ranch in the
last of the light, and saying how pretty my stock was,
and how he admired the build of my corrals and outbuildings. So the front porch is as far as any of them
got. You want to come up and help me decide about
that hay?"

Faro followed her up the rickety ladder, reflecting
that Jim McGree had been right about his prospects
not being endangered by Dora's imminent marriage
—but apparently dead wrong about the McGree property falling into his lap. He doubted that Alex McGree
would dare, even in death, to thwart his granddaughter's calm assumption of her right to succeed to it.

Jim was also off on another topic, Faro realized,
glancing up as Dora, above him, ascended the ladder,
skirts slightly hiked up. She might not be as opulently
built as some might like, but her curves were more
than respectable, and the walking-beam motion of her
buttocks under the dress fabric as she set foot on
alternate rungs, was suddenly exciting.

The hayloft was dim and filled with a pungent,
sweet-sharp smell from the depleted supply of last
year's hay. Dora knelt, straining the dress across her
thighs, bottom and back, and inspected a handful of
hay from the bottom of a pile. "Hasn't spoiled," she
said. "Good. I'll check it toward the back and corners.
You want to take one side—just dig in toward the bottom and see if it smells bad or's wet."

She scrambled over the heap of hay and vanished
behind it. Faro made his way to the rear of the loft
and probed. As far as he could tell, the hay looked
like hay, and no alarming stinks to it. It also acted
like hay, sending sharp bits into the crevices of his
coat, vest and shirt. By the time he returned to the

front of the loft, the invasion had spread to his trousers.

He had his shirt collar loosened and was trying to extract some of the itchier hay particles from around his neck when Dora returned. She slid down the face of the hay and lay back on it. "Seems fine," she said. "I'll just have the hands fork it toward the front and work the new crop in behind it, so the old'll get used first, come winter. Gets awful dry, doesn't it?" She brushed at the top of her dress, then lifted the neckline and blew down it. "Hay dander itches something awful."

"It does that," Faro said.

"But lying down on hay's so comfortable," she went on dreamily. "Sometimes I'll come up here to read or just be by myself and just sink into the hay. But then I'm hay all over, inside my clothes and out, so's I can hardly stand it. Know what I do then?"

"No, I don't," Faro said. "But I expect I would be interested to find out." It seemed to him that Reid might disapprove of what seemed to be shaping up, as complicating the investigation he was supposed to be making; but what Reid didn't know wouldn't hurt him. Also, a thorough investigation should explore every avenue, shouldn't it?—and it seemed to him that he was encountering some road signs pointing toward an avenue damned well worth exploring.

"Why, I just shuck my dress, and then I brush all the hay wisps and seeds off it," Dora said. "And then I kind of scrub myself down with it, so's to get all the hay off me."

Faro pictured the scene. "That would do the job," he said. What he visualized—Dora, pale and silky in the shadowed loft, going over every inch of her ripe body with the rolled-up dress—was very nearly doing the full job for him, so to speak. His trousers seemed to have shrunk at least two sizes, at least around the crotch, and he was itching with a good deal more than hay dander. "I don't know whether it'd be more fun lying down in the hay and getting all the comfort of it you spoke of, or that business about getting cleaned off after," he said.

"You won't be here but a short time, Cousin Sam," Dora said softly, "so I don't see that you'll have a great lot of chances to find out."

Faro settled onto the slanting wall of hay, next to her. "It is as springy as any down mattress," he admitted, "but the sharp points to it do dig in, so that you can't rightly settle down, and have to keep shifting about some."

"Mmm, that's right." Dora was moving slightly but constantly too, and the accidents of motion and the configuration of the haystack somehow set the gingham of her dress rubbing against the broadcloth of Faro's coat and trousers.

Faro turned to her, blew a finger-long strand of hay away from her face, and kissed her, hard and deep. Now, Captain, he told an invisible Reid, I got to take this opportunity to find out whatever I can from this prime source of McGree information, as was detailed in your personal orders, don't I? And if it don't come out that what develops is what you're after, then you can go fuck yourself. I personally have better prospects in that line.

By this time, the row of cloth-covered buttons down the front of Dora's dress were clear of their button-holes, and Faro was proving to himself that her breasts felt even better than they had looked yesterday, and, for a man with an educated tongue, tasted better than that.

Faro's coat had now mysteriously ascended to a rafter, from which it dangled like the corpse of a shot-gunned crow; his trousers had somehow worked their way down to his knees, and he was awkwardly astride but expertly into Dora McGree, whose blue dress lay bunched about her midriff as if it had decided that no matter what her percolating breasts, straining thighs, and receiving cunt were getting up to, a well-made garment ought to guard to the last against the exposure of its wearer's belly-button.

Faro's ultimate thrust brought Dora's thighs clamping about his haunches, and drove them both deep into the pile of hay. Faro came out of his state of happy shock to find himself dazed and almost dangerously choking on hay dust. He lay plastered to her for a moment, then, at the same time she did, made urgent swimming motions to clear from above them the weight of the hay, which had gently folded forward onto them until Faro had the alarmed thought that he was undergoing a vegetable avalanche.

"Well, Cousin Sam," Dora said, sitting up.

"Touching on that cousin business," Faro said, suddenly horrified that he might have drawn an untutored girl into committing what she thought was the sin of incest—

"There are cousins and there are cousins," Dora said flatly. "*Name* cousins, such as that Jim McGree, that is the degrees of kin that Scripture takes on about with forbiddings all over the place, and even a hand-shake that lasts overlong putting up the odds on hell-fire. But no-name cousins—I mean, people that are kin to kin to kin, such as the Jenkinses of the Carolinas stand to the McGrees of West Texas—why, they're not cousins at all, except under the statutes . . . and the statutes don't thicken things up around here very much, I will tell you."

"I guess I am glad to hear that," Faro said.

"Thought you would be," Dora commented. "Stand up and I'll brush some of the hay off where it's sticking to you."

Faro did, and, to his surprise, found that the hay-removing process led to something else entirely.

"Well, now, sort-of-cousin Sam," Dora, slick and warm and sliding against him and dodging off, said, "appears to me I've found a needle in a haystack."

Faro jerked under her questing fingers and said, "If that's your notion of a needle, I would guess you have some outlandish notions about what your warp and your woof is."

"Sam?"

"Hagh?"

"Just keep quiet, will you?"

When Faro left the barn, walking in a respectfully cousinly fashion after Dora, he was well aware that he had overlooked a number of opportunities to probe into the sort of things Reid would have wanted him to. He was also well aware that Reid, as far as he was concerned, could take a long walk off a short pier. A man that has got his ashes well and truly hauled, he reflected cheerfully, can afford to let the rest of the world go by without concerning himself overmuch as to the doings and mysteries of its inhabitants and denizens.

That was a good thought, and sound philosophy, he considered, looking into the westering sun. It didn't stay in place long, though, when confronted with the spectacle of four men lurching along with an awkward burden on a plank they carried, calling out hoarsely, "Some cocksucker's shot Owgooste!"

Faro ran toward the approaching men, remembering Shorty's words: "If there ain't no cook, there ain't no drive."

Chapter 7

By the time one of the hands had ridden the ten miles to San Bernardo and returned with the town medico, Owgooste had been cleansed of the blood that caked his arm, had the hasty bandage he had applied changed, and been settled in a spare bedroom.

"What the hell happened, Owgooste?" Alex McGree fretted, looking down at the wounded cook. Jim, Dora, and Faro were crowded around him.

"Well, I was out up north, toward the crick, boss, where there's a patch of woods I know that sometimes has some good mushrooms. I aimed to pick me a mess of 'em to dry an' take along on the drive. There ain't nothing like a handful of mushrooms to snap up a sonofabitch stew."

"What's that?" Faro asked.

Calf beef, heart, liver, sweetbreads, brains, marrow gut, spices. But it chust ain't the same without mushrooms."

"I don't expect it would be," Faro said thoughtfully.

"We ain't here to exchange recipes," Alex McGree said sharply. "Get on with it, Owgooste."

"Oh, yah. Well, I was looking for the mushrooms in them woods, boss. And I heard a horse, some ways away, and I thought it might be that mine had got loose from where I'd tied him, so I went to see, and chust as I come out of the woods there came a couple shots from close by, and I was flat on my ass with my arm hurting like shitfire—beg your pardon, Miss Dora."

"Never mind," Dora said. "You were and it was, so there's no harm in saying it."

"And then I tore a piece off of my shirt and tied it tight on the arm to stanch the bleeding and got to my horse and got onto it and pointed it toward the ranch house and then I passed out."

"You didn't see the fellow that shot you?" Jim asked.

"I didn't see much of nothing," Owgooste answered. "Chust the sky, when I was flat on my—on the ground, wondering what the hell had happened. I think I heard a horse riding off a little after."

"Well, we don't need a sighting to know who done the bushwhacking," Jim said grimly. "It's Holabird work, for sure."

"You can't know that!" Dora said indignantly. "Why would they want to do any such thing?"

"We're depending on the cash we're to get from this drive next week, honey," Alex McGree said sadly. "And short of running off all the stock, there ain't a better way to cripple a trail drive than taking out the cook. If Mal Holabird wants to ruin me, he couldn't have hit on a neater way to do it."

"Say, boss!" Owgooste said indignantly. "I ain't going to let a bullet stop me from cooking for the boys. It's through my stirring arm, yah, but you see, chust let the doc sew it up and slap some salve on it, and I'll be as good as new!"

The cook's words were slurred, and his face was bright and damp. Faro, studying him, concluded that the time for the drive would be long past before Owgooste would be doing any cooking.

Dr. Ash confirmed this after arriving and treating the patient. In the parlor, coatless, and with his up-turned shirtsleeves lightly flecked with blood, he accepted a tumbler of whiskey from Alex McGree and said, "The bullet's out and the wound's cleaned and closed. The muscle is some torn up, but I don't believe the bone was injured. There's some fever I don't like, but on the whole I'd say he'll mend in not much above a month."

"A month is awful long, Jake," Alex McGree said mournfully.

The doctor looked at him sharply. "I had my fill of patching men up fast so they could get back into action a dozen and more years ago, Alex," he said. "I hated battlefield surgery then, and I'm not about to get back into it now. You pad your buckboard with plenty of quilts, load Owgooste into it, and fetch him into town tomorrow morning. I'll put him up in my infirmary where I can keep an eye on him—and you'll get him back when I say he's ready to come back, not when you take a notion you need him!"

"He has the right of it," Alex McGree sighed, after the doctor had left. "But without Owgooste, I am al-mighty fearful of something going wrong with the drive. The boys would pitch in to handle his chores, of course, but it's a chancy business at best, and there is no way they could be working in prime form without a cook. Was things different—" He sighed again. "—I would hold this herd and do another drive in the fall, and get Mal Holabird to see me through until then with a loan. But . . ."

"Well, you know, Cousin Alex," Jim said firmly, "that now he's showed himself in his true colors, that old thief'd lend you a bucket of coal in hell, but nothing more useful. I think we have got to start getting ready to deal with Mal Holabird and Bob Holabird and the rest of the whole damn nest of 'em once and for all. If you ain't sure the boys we have now have got the sand for that kind of work, there is some men I know of that could be wired to to see if they would care to lend a hand."

Faro looked at him with interest, wondering about the experience and background that might have provided Jim McGree with the information needed to reach free-lance gunmen by telegraph.

Alex McGree scowled at his cousin over his half-glasses, then brightened. "Now there is an idee! I don't mean bringing in fellows to side us in a war, for I don't propose to have that, no matter what Mal Holabird gets up to in his old age, nor Bob Holabird in his young age. But lending hands, sure. There is ranchers up in Montana and Wyoming that won't be moving their trail herds for a month or so yet, or might even be passing until it's time for the fall drive. I know some of them fellows, and it might could be that one of 'em wouldn't mind letting me have the loan of a trail cook for this drive. I will go into town with Owgooste tomorrow and send off a bunch of telegrams—could be, by nightfall I'll have the promise of one, and the whole problem'll be settled."

At first stony as his cousin had outlined his idea, Jim McGree's face had assumed an approving expression by the time Alex had finished. "Now, that is a thought," he said slowly. "A damn good way to show the Holabirds they can't buffalo the McGrees. But you shouldn't have to go into San Bernardo, Cousin Alex—there is Holabirds underfoot and overhead there, and if they was to get wind of what you're about, you'd be in danger of getting backshot. You give me the names and addresses, and write out in a fair hand what you want said, and I'll see to the telegraphing. I can get in and out of San Bernardo safe enough, long's I keep my eyes open, but the way things are going now, the head of the McGree clan would be too much of a temptation for those Holabird bastards."

Alex McGree looked forlornly at the floor, and said, "I haven't been into town since all this started up. San Bernardo ain't much of a place, but going in there once in a while made a change."

"Wouldn't be a good notion," Jim said firmly.

Faro spoke up: "Expect this peril you talk of don't apply overmuch to Jenkinses of South Carolina, McGree connections though they be. I would admire to go into town with you, Cousin Jim, and see Owgooste settled, maybe get a haircut, now that the Lazy M barber is non compos clippers or so."

Jim shrugged. "If you want to. Believe I'll turn in now. 'Night, Cousin Alex, Cousin Dora, Cousin Sam."

When he had left, Faro relaxed slightly. If Jim had come up with a plausible objection to Faro's company on the trip to town, it could have been awkward. For now, having talked to Alex and Dora McGree, and gauged the feelings of the cowhands, it seemed to him that the roots of the feud, whatever they might be, did not lie at the Lazy M. They might not lie in

San Bernardo either, but it could be worth looking there.

Also, if he could convince Reid that there was nothing out here worth watching for, maybe he would be allowed to hightail out of here without the tall Ranger setting him up for a lifetime on General Steele's shitlist.

He walked Dora to the stairs leading to the upper floor of the ranch house. "Any errands you want me to do for you in town?" he asked. "Stuff bought, or a message left with your friend Stella? I take it she don't hold with this feud, so I'd not be in any danger from her."

Dora gave him an amused smile. "You might be—depends what you mean by danger—if she was there. She's visiting family out in California, expected back some time next week. And no, I don't need anything from town, thanks."

They were now at the head of the stairs, in the center of the corridor onto which the big house's several bedrooms opened.

"My room's at the far left end," Faro said.

"I know. It was me that picked it," she said.

"I don't know where yours is."

"Nor you don't," she agreed cheerfully.

"Ah . . ."

"And it's not your concern," she went on. "A hay-loft is one thing, my grandpa's house is another. It wouldn't be fitting to shame him under his roof. So good night, Cousin Sam."

Shrugging into his nightshirt a few moments later, Faro tried to work out the logic behind Dora's compunctions, and gave it up. Men's minds and women's, he guessed, just naturally worked differently. Men dealt with hard facts and logic, like a full house being ranked by four of a kind, but women invented their own rules.

"Was I you, Marshal," Jim McGree said, "I would have every one of them murdering Holabirds behind bars by now."

"Was you me," Pratt said flatly, "you would then be pretty soon on your way to Austin in irons, as having gone plumb crazy and exceeded your lawful authority by a good bit too long a sight."

"There's dead men and wounded, and the Holabirds behind it all!" Jim argued.

"That cook fellow you just brung in," the marshal said, "can't put a name nor a shape, even, to who shot him. And there's no name, nor much of a shape left, to the fellow that got blowed up down by the river day before yestiddy, and no way to know who fired the shot that done it. My own opinion," he added, "is that a man that takes shelter from gunfire behind kegs that is plainly marked BLASTING POWDER—HIGH EXPLOSIVE can't read, so I am treating the case as death by illiteracy, which is more natural causes than crime."

The marshal tilted back in his chair. "I will admit," he said, "that there has been unlawful happenings piling up considerable of late. And I will admit that talk runs high amongst the Holabirds and them that work for them against the McGrees, and topsy turvy. But I ain't yet seen a McGree clearly identified with some damage to a Holabird man or Holabird property, nor a Holabird viewed by witnesses where McGree things or people has sustained damage."

"Well, Jesus, Marshal," Jim said in disgust, "it's plain as day. The Holabirds is just too crafty to be seen about their work against us, and it's them as well that's pretending to do hurt to their own side, so's to give us McGrees a bad name. I don't say that Bob Holabird himself burnt them ricks out on the Lazy M last month, for he's too yellow to take a hand in such as that, but you can bet he ordered it done, or old Mal did. And then they turned around and looted their own warehouse, and tried to put it on us, and so with all the rest of it."

"For a long time," the marshal said slowly, "Mc-Grees and Holabirds come down very strict for law and order around here. It takes some studying for me to work out how they are now busting it up."

"Old Mal Holabird's been living for years with the shame of that Mex treasure he stole from Cousin Alex," Jim said impatiently. "It's worked on his mind so that he's started to spread lies that Cousin Alex took it, and to back the lie he's faked crimes against his own property and people, and done real ones against ours."

"There is talk," Pratt said, "that some of that stuff has been done by Louse Pointers, and not McGrees nor Holabirds at all."

"Well, now, ain't that a easy answer?" Jim said heavily. "Put it all onto Louse Point. High-spirited fellows ride out of there and burn a rick or shoot a cook just so as to pass the time before their next number of *Godey's Ladies' Book* comes in the mail. If you got the notion that Louse Point is behind all this—lemme say, if the Holabirds has given you that notion—why don't you just go in there and clean it out?"

"You know that I don't have jurisdiction in Louse Point, nor does no other U.S. law officer," Pratt said.

"The shit you been handing us, Marshal, I would doubt you got jurisdiction over your own asshole,"

Jim said. "Now, I am asking you, all formal, on behalf of Mr. Alex McGree of the Lazy M, just what you are doing about this."

To Faro's surprise, Pratt did not react at all strongly to Jim's tirade, but merely said blandly, "The situation's in hand, Mr. McGree. I am in consultation with the due authorities, and will be discussing it with them shortly—this very day, in fact." As he spoke, he looked straight at Faro and let one eyelid, unseen by Jim, droop meaningfully.

"While as you are consulting and discussing, I will be doing what I can to make sure the Holabirds' dastardly attack on poor Owgooste don't ruin Cousin Alex entirely," Jim said bitterly. "I will get on to the telegraph office and start wiring out to the ranchers he wants to be in touch with for a spare cook. Coming, Cousin Sam?"

Marshal Pratt casually raised one hand to screen his face from Jim, though not from Faro, and contorted it vigorously.

Faro, hoping he had read the lawman's message aright, said, "Uh . . . no. Might not be much point to it, but I would like to make a complaint to the marshal here about that jasper that roughed me up the other day. If we can stick one of them Holabird people with even a teensy thing like assault, it couldn't hurt. So I'll stick around here a bit and get the marshal going on the paperwork. Meet you in the Catamount in a while, okay?"

Jim nodded his assent and left. When he was well away from the office, Marshal Pratt nodded and said, "Glad you caught on, Blake. When Doc Ash gave me word about Owgooste being shot, and having to be brought into town, Reid figured you'd find a way to come along, and was particular anxious to have some time with you."

"And so I am," the Ranger captain said, stepping in from the office's rear door. "And here's another man I think you and I have better talk with." He gestured behind him at a tall, white-haired, hawk-nosed individual in a dark-brown broadcloth suit. "Mr. Mal Holabird."

"I never truly held it against him," Holabird was saying a few moments later. "Enough money to tempt any man, and Alex could use it, right then, for fair, him being in the way of getting started. I won't deny that if it'd been me in the boat with Locksley when the Mexes killed him and sunk it, I'd have thought hard about whether I couldn't use it all myself instead of sharing it out, as had been agreed. By luck, a couple hundred dollars I'd put into California land gave me a claim on some creeks that turned out to be just about running with gold a few years later, so I didn't have to grudge him the money. But I couldn't, d'you see, be as close to him after he did that as I was before—we did business together, though I took extra care to see that everything was clear, legal and binding, not trusting as I would have in his handshake—but real friendliness, that we had as young men, why, that had to go by the board."

Pratt's eyes seemed slightly glazed, as though he had heard Holabird's disquisition before. So had Faro —only, in barely different terms, from Alex McGree.

"But now, I believe he's begun to die at the top, like a tree," Holabird went on. "He knows he wronged me, and the others that would have shared that Mexican treasure, and he wants to get shut of that somehow before he goes to his grave, so he's putting the guilt of it on me, and riling up this feud to make it convincing."

Faro had heard this last argument quite recently, but was not, as Pratt had been, bored by the repetition—it was remarkably close to Jim McGree's version of Holabird's motives.

"Well, we'll see what we can do about putting a stop to it," Reid said, when Holabird had finished. "Thanks very much, Mr. Holabird, for telling us how things look from your side."

As Pratt ushered him out of the office's rear entrance, Mal Holabird looked back at Faro and the Ranger. "If you can get that old knothead Alex McGree to call this off, I'll go along," he said. "For peace, and maybe old times' sake, I'll write off the looting and the badmouthing he's done. And if he needs some cash to tide him over, along of his plans for the spring drive coming asunder, I'd not deny him any reasonable loan he asked for."

"Now, that's a interesting situation," Faro said when the marshal returned and joined him and Reid. "There's two bunches of men that's out for each other's blood and bowels, and the head of each of them bunches is feeling wronged and regretful about the whole shebang. Like you said, Reid, it don't have the smell of one of your everyday feuds."

"Something else," Reid said thoughtfully. "The McGree story is that Holabird was in the boat with Locksley and the treasure, and the McGrees say that Holabird was. But until both of them turned up their starting money a little later, the idea was that Locksley had been alone—that he was killed, and the treasure lost in the river. Now, look into that a little more closely, see what it really is—no Locksley, no treasure—and it seems to me that you could come up with a different answer."

"Locksley alive and the treasure not so much sunk as absconded," Faro said. "So that Holabird and McGree could be right in suspicioning the whole deal, but wrong as to the bottom dealer."

"But that just gets you to where them two don't trust each other overmuch," Pratt interposed, "and don't bear much on the clear and present situation, which is how whatsoever was wrong betwixt 'em has commenced to fester and develop maggots. Has one or both of 'em started to go soft, the way each of 'em is suggesting about the other?"

"Would you say Mal Holabird's wits were loose from their mooring?" Reid asked the marshal, who gave a negative shake of his head.

"And there ain't no signs of crown rot as I can see in Alex McGree," Faro said. The happy vision of the case being cleared up enough so that Reid would cheerfully dispense with his presence had by now vanished, and he was resigned to seeing it through. In a way, he didn't regret the compulsion: he had come to like old Alex McGree and Dora, and while it wouldn't have been businesslike or his common practice to stick around and help them out because of that liking, he could now tell himself that he was being forced to, which made it all right, or almost.

The three-man conference broke up with no new plans made. Faro, anticipating a longer stay in San Bernardo than he had envisioned, strolled down to the Western Union office, and entered the frame building. He had recalled that the 1877 number of the E. N. Grandine catalogue was due out earlier this month, and decided to wire the New York firm to send it on to him. Grandine was the most reliable and inventive supplier of "advantage tools"—the card sharp's armamentarium of cheating devices—and Faro studied each year's edition with devout concentration. His main interest was to see what new inventions had come along so as to be prepared to encounter them in a game; but it usually happened each year that Grandine came up with something he felt it prudent to include in his own tool case.

"I ain't that sure of the address," he told the clerk, "but—"

"Western Union office in New York could find it quick as winking," the young man behind the desk said. "However, the problem doesn't arise just now." He gestured behind him toward the spidery brass-and-steel instrument which stood uncharacteristically silent. "The line's been out since early this morning. I expect it'll be back in service in a day or so."

"What happened?" Faro asked.

The clerk shrugged. "That I won't know until it's working again and I get told. Once the line is down, it could be that anything happened, up to everything fifty miles west of here and fifty miles east being consumed by volcanoes, though I personally doubt that. Going by past experience, I'd say it was Apaches."

"Cutting the line so's we wouldn't get any warning of a raid?" Faro asked, uneasily aware of the Lazy M's isolation and vulnerability.

"Naw, jewelry," the clerk said. "They got this notion that if the wire can carry messages from here to Washington or 'Frisco in an eyeblink, it has got to be pretty strong stuff, so that half a fathom of it wound around a man's wrist would make him extra powerful or lucky, which they count as the same thing. Also, it shines nice, being high-grade copper, which is a consideration with your Indian. So, time to time, they chop out a length of it and go off, and a crew has to come out, find the break, and trace it. The company'll have had a crew start out soon's the line went dead, and I expect we'll be back in business tomorrow morning, latest, maybe sooner."

Faro thanked the clerk and left, damning the vanity and credulity of the red man, not so much over the frustration of his own minor message as over the delay this would already have caused in Jim's wired quest for a cook to replace Owgooste. Even a day's wait now could be dangerous for Alex McGree.

He found Jim wolfing a plate of steak and beans, which represented the height of the Catamount's cuisine—the saloon served as San Bernardo's only restaurant and its nearest approximation to a hotel.

"Hey, Cousin Sam." Jim waved a leathery piece of meat speared on the end of his fork at Faro. "Change of plans. I'm staying in San Bernardo tonight, not going back to the ranch. You want to stay in with me or take the buckboard on back and send it in tomorrow with one of the hands?"

"I'd as soon stay," Faro said, "so long's the Catamount can find me a room. This because of that telegram business?" It made sense for Jim to want to stick around until the messages to Alex McGree's rancher friends had gone out and had a chance to be replied to.

"Sure thing. It came to me, once I'd handed 'em in at the office, that the answers likely wouldn't be back today, and I'd as soon go back to Cousin Alex with real news, whether good or bad."

"But the main thing for now is, they went out," Faro said slowly.

Jim nodded. "All eight of 'em, tapped off most

brisk and efficient. It's a wonder what electricity can do."

"Yeah. They tell me even electric wire, if wore as a bracelet, has remarkable powers," Faro said. "I will go get me a drink and see about renting a room for myself here."

As he made his way to the bar, he was studying this new nugget of information with care and interest. The line had gone out at about the time Owgooste was being loaded into the bucket for the haul into San Bernardo. And that meant that Jim McGree hadn't set foot in the telegraph office at all today, if he were unaware of it.

And that in turn meant that Jim McGree would be a very damned good man to keep an eye on. For, if he had never intended to send the telegrams that might be the salvation of Alex McGree's trail drive and so of Alex McGree's ranch, which side was he on in this McGree-Holabird mess?

Chapter 8

"Now, that is what you call a real clue," Reid said. "That telegram business, that is real interesting."

"I thank you," Faro said. He and the Ranger were sitting at a rear table in the Catamount, which was now about half-filled. For a place like this in a town like this, Faro thought, it had a decidedly sparse showing of cowboys; he put this circumstance down to the effects of the McGree-Holabird feud, which as he had already heard, tended to keep Shorty and his boys out of town.

"And Jim McGree's turned in?"

"Half an hour ago, about nine," Faro said. "Said he wanted to be fresh and rested if there was to be negotiations done over the telegraph tomorrow concerning any cook hirings."

"Well, what time he gets up, you stick to him like a mustard plaster," Reid said, filling his glass from a bottle he had, somewhat to Faro's irritation, kept to himself, and half-draining it. "I will stick to Bob Holabird like a mustard plaster as well. So they'll both be plastered, hey?"

"Not so much as some other folks not a thousand miles from here," Faro said, watching the Ranger refill his glass. "I thought you kept off the booze owing to its effect on the system and health in general."

"And so I do," Reid said. "This here is cold tea that I got the barkeep to make up for me and dispense under the strictest of secrecy, which is why I haven't been sharing it out with you. The very color and look of good whiskey, but none of the bad side of it. I just top it up with some of the Sachem's Bitters—" He tilted some of the elixir from the flat bottle into the glass and stirred it in with his forefinger. "—and I am set."

"So you are," Faro said, watching the Ranger take in a mouthful of tea, alcohol and opium that would have gained the respect of a *yen shee gow* addict at Tsai Wang's place in San Francisco. "So, as I see it, my sticking don't start until morning, when Jim takes the notion to end his beauty sleep. What about yours?"

"I am into it," Reid said. "See that long, tall sort of a fellow over by the bar?" Faro looked in the direction the Ranger indicated, and saw a lean six-plus-footer sporting the same eagle beak that Mal Holabird had displayed; three or four shorter—that is to say, average-height—men clustered around him. "That is Bob Holabird," Reid went on, "so if he's here and I'm here, that is about as much sticking or plastering as you can get into. It's a treat, I'll tell you, to sit here, nights, and listen to him sounding off on what he'll do to the McGrees, paying special attention to Jim, that he'd admire to twist the extremities off of. He gets a good hand from the audience when he comes out with those sentiments, but I would guess that it's as much because he's buying drinks all around as that the opinion is general."

It seemed to Faro that the Catamount was having a dull evening—maybe, he thought, all its evenings were dull, and no wonder. The only event of any interest took place during Reid's brief absence to empty his bladder of cold tea and tonic. A roughly dressed man came up to Holabird, drew his attention with a gesture, mouthed a few words into his ear, and left the saloon. So, after a moment, did Bob Holabird.

"Hell and Maria," Reid said, when, upon his return, Faro told him of this, "why didn't you follow him and see where he went?"

"I got the mustard-plastering of Jim," Faro pointed out. "Bob is yours."

"Hey, thass right," Reid said. "You plaster your mustard, I'll plaster mine. Given time, Bob'll bob up bob up bob up bob bob bob."

The Ranger's eyes were open but unfocused; apparently, Faro thought, he hadn't managed to piss away the important elements of the Sachem's Bitters, and could be counted out of whatever else might be happening this evening.

The thought reminded him that his own intake, though not as exotic as Reid's, had been just as fluid, and was beginning to present him with an urgency. He rose and headed for the saloon's rear door.

Faro gave a silent sigh as he flicked the last drop from the end of his penis and tucked it into his trousers.

He was standing in the darkness at the back wall of the Catamount, and ready to return to the saloon for a last drink—and, perhaps, to see that Reid made it to wherever he was supposed to be lodged. As he worked on his trouser buttons, he saw a flicker of shadow against the light washing in from the main street. He ran to the edge of the building and peered down the street.

The stocky figure could have belonged to any of a number of the denizens of San Bernardo. But the last glow from the front windows of the Catamount picked out the face of Jim McGree.

Who was, as Faro was aware, advertised and warranted to be asleep in his rented room.

I had figured on this mustard-plastering starting in about breakfast time, Faro complained inwardly. But if that Ranger has managed to lose track of his man before midnight, I guess I had better hump myself to keep mine in sight.

Down the moonlit, deserted street, keeping to the shadows of the buildings, he followed.

Jim McGree's destination turned out to be the rickety pier that jutted out into the river. He climbed down from it into a dark oblong that bobbed on the silvered water of the river, then poled away from the shore.

Faro waited a moment, then walked to the pier, clambered down into a skiff that was moored to it, and loosed the craft's lines. It had a short mast with a furled sail, like Jim's, but Faro had no notion of how to employ it, and in any case, there seemed to be a fairly steady upriver breeze. He decided to follow Jim's example and drift downriver with the current, and used the single oar to propel the boat into midstream. The Rio Grande's current caught him, as it had Jim McGree, and sent him at about the speed of a fast horse toward the Gulf of Mexico.

He was dubious about his chances of following Jim on the return trip, presuming that his quarry would use sail—doubtless something would occur to him to get around that.

The moon was well away from being full, but it was bright and high in the cloudless sky, and the Rio Grande, from Mexican to American shore, shone like hammered metal. Out of old habit, Faro looked behind him, and saw the empty, glittering river—if Jim McGree has them kind of instincts, he thought, I am at the end of my string.

But it seemed to him that the hunched figure in the skiff ahead had not turned to survey what lay behind it. Cousin Jim is just not a ass-coverer by nature, Faro thought—elsewise he'd not have let himself get caught out so on that Western Union business.

A few times, Faro's skiff seemed to fall behind Jim's, or to drift toward the Mexican shore. At such moments, he plied the oar vigorously until the condition was corrected; but for the most part he had little to do but let the great river take the boat and its lone passenger where it would.

Memories came to him of moonlight on other rivers: the Mississippi, where he—his voice not yet cracking—his father, and Doc Prentiss had studied the curious ways of professional gamblers; the Missouri, snaking farther up into the badlands than anybody would have expected; and the broad Hudson, the time he'd been east and gone north of New York City to visit that railroad man's daughter. I keep breath in me long enough, he thought, and maybe I will get to see the Amazon and the Thames and the Rhine and the Volga—all the other big rivers.

Jim McGree's skiff angled in toward the left bank of the river. The distance downstream from San Bernardo, the dim fuzz of light from a few scattered sources, and a raucous medley of cries and music served to tell what his destination—and Faro's—must be.

Louse Point.

Faro felt for the pistol-knuckleduster in his vest pocket, and wished he had the cutdown shotgun along.

Ten minutes later, having followed Jim McGree up from the waterfront to the derelict buildings of Louse Point, and having stepped over one recent corpse and turned aside offers of cut-rate hashish and opium, Faro paused under the crumbling walls of the old Mexican fort. Jim had gone into a two-story building across the way, which, from the light, music and noise which poured from it had to be the center of what nightlife Louse Point offered.

He decided to wait a few minutes, then make a cautious entrance; it wouldn't do for Jim to spot him if he could avoid it. In spite of the heat of the evening, the old stones of the fort seemed to exude a dank cold; and he remembered that here was where Mal Holabird, Alex McGree and the elusive Locksley had staged their invasion of what was then Mexican territory.

"Waiting for somebody, Mister? I c'n show you a good time."

The hoarse query from the woman who had lurched up to him was familiar. Her costume, which consisted of no more than a pair of run-over shoes, was not.

"Well, no, thank you," Faro said. "I got business elsewheres."

"Right up against the wall here for a dollar—fifty cents, if you're in a hurry," the woman said. She was plump, with pointed breasts jutting out almost at right angles to each other. On one breast, and her belly and knees, were smears of earth; Faro supposed that she had recently fallen in the roadway, or serviced her last client face down and outdoors.

"Like I said, I am busy, but here's a half dollar for luck." Faro tossed her the coin and watched her walk away, backside jiggling. He was hoping to see where she proposed to stow her unearned fee, as she carried no purse, but his attention was distracted by a coughing laugh from almost beneath his feet.

"Lucy surprise you some?" what looked like a bundle of rags against the wall said.

"Most places, the whores keep their clothes on outside their places of business," Faro said. "Constable'd run 'em in, otherwise."

"Lucy's place of business is right under her belly, friend," the squatting derelict croaked. "And there's no constables in Louse Point, d'you see? So who's to tell Lucy to cover herself up? You c'n go bareass here, or drunk, or crazy, and nobody'll lock you up for it. American law nor Mex don't run here, so it's a place whereat a man can be free."

"Lucy's prices come pretty close to that," Faro said. "Fifty cents ain't much even for a fast standing poke."

"Around here, there is enough women that gives it away so that the market price ain't high," the bum said. "Plus, if a man is inclined to take without payin', there is no jailin' nor hangin' into it, and only the risk of misusin' a woman that some feller with a short temper and a long trigger finger thinks well of."

Faro decided that it was time to sample Louse Point's high society on his own. "Obliged to you for the chat," he told the derelict, and flipped a quarter to him. To his surprise, the man did not stir to pick it up from the ground.

"I will tell you," the bum said thoughtfully, "I

would appreciate if you would have somebody acrost the way, if as you're goin' in there, fetch me out whatever kind of drink you'd care to buy me. See, if I was to go in there and buy my own with silver, there is those as'd figure I had more on me, and would come and kill me for it. They'd be fooled, accourse, but that wouldn't do me no good."

Faro considered this last illustration of the perfect freedom of life without law in Louse Point, gave the requested promise, and entered the establishment across from the fort's ruins.

The place was brightly lit, noisy, reeking of tobacco smoke and liquor fumes, and seemed to combine in one room the main attractions of a saloon, a gambling hell, a dance hall, and a whorehouse. Keeping an eye out for Jim McGree but not seeing him, he worked his way over to the bar and told one of the several men lounging behind it to take a pint of cheap wine across the street.

"Old Gummy," the man said, accepting Faro's payment for the service. "He don't care much to come in here since the first time. He flashed some gold, and some of the boys took it right away from him."

"Gummy?" Faro asked. "How'd he come by that name?"

"It was gold *teeth,* the front ones," the man said. "Had 'em out faster than Painless Parker, only without the painless part, a gunbutt bein' employed instead of the usual forceps."

Gummy's needs seen to, Faro secured a drink for himself and drifted to what he hoped was an inconspicuous corner of the bar, still looking for Jim McGree.

He was on his second drink before he saw his man. Jim was descending a staircase in company with another man. They paused, seemed to argue, then turned and went back upstairs. Their interchange seemed to Faro to have had more the nature of a business discussion than an argument, a discussion which they apparently meant to continue.

What made this ordinary-appearing encounter strangely interesting to Faro was the identity of Jim McGree's companion—his sworn and deadly enemy, Bob Holabird.

Chapter 9

Well, now, Faro told himself, it looks like Bob escaped
Captain Reid's mustard-plastering. So it's for me to
stick to 'em both for the moment, and with Jim at the
least when he heads back for San Bernardo or wherever.

He considered how to pass the time until Jim Mc-
Gree should reappear. At the bar, he would be too
easily spotted from the staircase. The far corner of the
room would give him an early view of anyone descending it without exposing him dangerously; that
would be the place.

He made his way there. The central feature of this
area was a waist-high table on which a well-attended
crap game was in progress. Faro watched it for a
while, and, somewhat to his surprise, the fall of the
dice seemed pretty much according to the laws of
chance. In Louse Point, of all places, he would have
expected the ivories to be shaved or loaded. He con-

firmed his impression by moving into the game and giving them a covert inspection.

After a moment, he nodded; it figured. Crooked gambling depended on there being some kind of law somewhere in the background. Here, any suspicion of fast work, even, would be a one-way ticket across Jordan for the man who tried it, with his killer likely being given a general round of applause and being stood to drinks. For a man who wanted absolutely and totally honest gambling, it looked as though Louse Point was the place to visit.

Faro made his point, five, collected his modest winnings, and stood back, letting someone else take over as shooter while he concentrated on side bets for a while. He noted that the Louse Point crap enthusiasts had a weakness for place bets, favoring the 4-10 and 5-9 combinations—that is, they would win, at substantial odds, any time one of these numbers came up, regardless of whether it was the shooter's point. Which, in Faro's experience, meant that they were suckers: the house odds against them were deadly, and the payoff came nowhere near reflecting that. He contented himself with line bets, either pass—with the shooter—or don't-pass.

Craps was not his game, but he knew it well enough to get into its tempo after a while, to vary his bets as he sensed the ebb and flow of the shooter's luck; and he soon had a sizeable pile of winnings in front of him. As a professional gambler, Faro had little of what is called the gambling instinct in him; he made his living by an absolute knowledge of the odds and a near-absolute knowledge of the frailties and failings of the men who played against him. There were times, though, when he had a sense of something way off-stage clicking together and seeing to it that Faro Blake was due for something a little better than house odds for a few minutes, and, more often than not, when he'd let that sense have its way, he'd come out ahead.

One such moment was on him now, an almost physical tingling in his fingers. If he was ever going to have an outstanding run with the dice, it would be tonight. Anyhow, he was enough ahead so that if his sense of luck had played him false, he could curtail his play without having lost much.

He took over as shooter and rolled the dice. They fetched up against the backboard and displayed one dot each—snake-eyes. So much for luck.

"Cocked dice," the stickman said. "Take it over." Faro now noticed that one baleful snake-eye was resting at an angle against the backboard.

This time the roll was a seven, and he added to his winnings. Then a four, which he made in three passes. He was breathing a little faster, and had to keep reminding himself to keep an eye on the rear staircase. He was tempted to let all his winnings ride on each pass, but prudently transferred a good portion of them to his pockets.

A scent of musk came to him. "You're rolling lucky," a husky voice said. He turned and looked at the woman who had drifted up to stand next to him. She was wearing a good bit more than Lucy, which still left her in a state that would have subjected her to instant arrest any place outside of a ladies' Turkish bath or Louse Point.

"I am that," Faro said.

"You want to make sure of your luck?" she asked.

"Who wouldn't?" Faro rolled a six.

"Two dollars."

From the attitude of those around him, he gathered that this was a customary exaction. "Well, hell."

He handed her two coins from the pile in front of him and rolled again. A six, and he raked in more winnings.

"I guess you brung me luck, all—" he started to say to the woman, but saw that she had vanished. He took up the dice for the next roll, then realized that something damned strange was happening to the front of his trousers. He bent and peered under the table and saw the woman crouched beneath it, her fingers working at his fly buttons.

"What the hell?" he said.

Her response of "Luck" did not enlighten him.

"You better come out of there," he muttered fiercely. "People'll see you."

"They see me all the time here. I French a man while he's rolling, he has good luck, it's a known fact." She had his penis free of his trousers now, and was briskly rolling it between her palms.

"Well, thank you, but I ain't interested in the service," Faro said, still in a low voice.

She flicked his now-distended shaft with a forefinger. "Seems to me you are. Anyhow, you paid me, so I got to deliver. Might's well get back to the dice."

Faro straightened up and gave the bystanders a weak smile. It was plain that he could take no further action to repel the woman without creating a scene which would attract unwelcome attention to him. He twitched as he felt her lips take in the head of his penis, and addressed himself once more to the dice.

He rolled an eleven for a win; then, on a hunch, left only the minimum bet down on his next pass, crapping out with a twelve.

Maybe there is something in this, he thought. He was fully erect now, and she was halfway up him, her tongue sliding back and forth across the underside of his shaft. Given the way things are in Louse Point, it's no more unusual than anything else. But I would give a pretty to know how a tradition like that come to be started. . . .

Successive rolls enriched Faro and those bettors who stayed with him on the pass line. As dice rattled and piles of coins were shoved across the green baize surface of the table, remarkable things were happening beneath it. The woman's lips were grazing on his pubic hair now; by Faro's estimation, she had to have taken him in well down her throat. She was warm and tight and sliding around him, and he was finding it harder to concentrate on the dice.

He made three more points, suspected he was due for craps, reduced his stake again, and threw a two. Now he could feel the power returning to his fingers, *knew* he would make the next point, and rolled. Four. The woman moved on him in slow, urgent rhythm. His fingers were alive, and so was his cock; the rest of him seemed a kind of void. Three. Then an eight that for an instant looked as though it were going to turn up seven and crap him out.

He picked up the dice once more and readied himself to roll. Then three things happened at once: Jim McGree appeared on the staircase; Faro rolled a winning four; and his cock pulsed and exploded, wrenching him with a sudden spasm.

He braced himself on the table with both arms, breathing heavily and looking downward for a moment, partly to conceal his face from Jim McGree, partly because he felt kitten-weak and found his head difficult to support.

The woman grunted and pulled away from him. Faro swept his winnings from the table, pushed himself into his trousers and rebuttoned the fly, and relinquished the dice to the next shooter.

He bent down and looked under the table. The woman was still crouched there. He handed her a fistful of silver dollars and said, "Thanks for the luck."

He straightened and saw Jim McGree's back vanishing through the doorway. Faro moved after him, walking clumsily with the weight of his winnings, distributed in coat and trousers pockets, throwing him a little off stride.

He peered out of the doorway and saw McGree striding past the ruins of the fort, in the direction of the landing.

Faro waited until his quarry was almost out of sight, then followed him. The noise of the place he had just left faded behind him, and Louse Point at this hour—it was now, he supposed, well past midnight—was unaccustomedly quiet; the loudest sound he heard was the jingling of coins in his pockets. He thought he heard the sound of running feet off to his left, but that faded quickly.

The rudimentary street took a sharp left turn just ahead, and he quickened his pace—he was expecting Jim to make for the landing, but that was no guarantee that he'd do as expected. He might cut in any direction, or—Faro paused—have spotted that he was being followed and be waiting at the corner to surprise his pursuer.

Faro poked his head around the corner of a hovel. Jim McGree wasn't waiting for him. Three other men were, though, one of them with a club which took him clumsily but effectively on the side of the head, sending him sprawling to the ground.

He retched as a boot toe caught him in the pit of the stomach, grabbed at the leg that had propelled it, and heaved. One attacker yelled and went sprawling.

"Kick the sonofabitch in the haid," one of the others advised.

"Kick him in the balls," his companion said.

While Faro was deciding which target to try to protect, both were hit at once. The burst of pain in his groin made him almost grateful for the efficiency of the head kick, which sent him spinning into the dark.

I hope, he thought distractedly as unconsciousness claimed him, that these fellows are after my winnings. If they're Jim McGree's men, I misdoubt I'll be waking up. . . .

"Oh, shit."

"Well, how was I to know? I don't keep a picture gallery of every man hereabouts 'in my head. Never *occurred* to me he come from San Bernardo."

Faro came awake to find an argument in progress among his assailants. He also discovered that he was tightly trussed, hand and foot, gagged, and lying· in the corner of a stone-floored room lit by a single candle. From the fact that one corner of the room stood open to the night sky, he deduced that he was in the ruined fort.

"You ain't been in San Bernardo in a month. I was there yestiddy and seed this jasper in the Catamount. *And* hobnobbing with Jim, to boot."

"Oh, shit."

"You know how Jim and Bob are on that. How we handle things amongst ourselves is our business, so long as it's only Pointers involved. But it's hands off anybody from the outside, unless either of 'em gives the word—that stuff about the law not coming in here works only so long as there ain't too much of a fuss

111

raised about it. Jim and Bob ain't neither one going to be almighty pleased about this."

"You was in it just as much as we was—how come you didn't stop us when you seed who it was?"

"Because, you asshole, I didn't rightly get a look at him 'til after he was knocked out. All *I* knowed was, you two come boiling down to my shack, told me there was a big winner leaving the place, and we could take him, easy. Easy it was, but I misdoubt we'll live awful long to enjoy the taking."

"Could we give him back his money an' say it was all a mistake, that we took him for somebodys else that we had a spite on?"

Faro silently but heartily seconded this proposal, but the man who seemed to be the leading spirit of the trio vetoed it firmly. "Nope. Jim'd come to know of it, and make an example of us—he don't cotton to mistakes. Rather than be made an example of by Jim or Bob, I tell you, I'd cut my throat and walk into the river. You remember what happened to Porky Henderson."

"Oh, shit," said the man whose vocabulary seemed to be confined to those two words; this time he used them with deep feeling.

"Then why don't we just corpse him an' sink him?"

"Because he's gonna be missed at San Bernardo, and it won't likely be much trouble to trace him here and figure him for the fellow that won big at dice. And when Jim and Bob start setting their minds to figure out who has a name for bushwhacking winners, you got any doubt which names'll crop up first?"

"Oh, shit."

"We can't turn this fellow loose to talk, and we can't do him in ourselves. We got to have somebody landed with the job to satisfy Jim and Bob. Old Pop Smol-lett."

"Shit, yeah!"

"Pop's mean enough to do it for fun, and so fuddled, nobody'll pay any attention to anything he might say about us setting him up. Jim and Bob don't like him being here, anyhow—he's too crazy for them—so they'll be primed to example him right quick."

"I hear Pop has did things in his time that'd give a 'Pache the dry heaves to look at. Word is, he was throwed out of Quantrill's Raiders for being too rough, and got meaner afterwards."

"Then he's our man, ain't he? All we got to do is go find Pop, let him know there's a fellow tied up in here that maybe has some money on him—we'd best leave a few cartwheels in his pockets—and Pop'll do the rest. Come morning, he'll be blind drunk on the pro-ceeds, this jasper'll be found with things done to him that only Pop'd think of doing, and it's all laid out neat. Likely he'll be exampled before he's had time to sober up."

The other two seemed to find no fault with the lead-er's plan; a handful of coins was slipped back into Faro's coat pocket as he lay feigning unconsciousness; and the trio exited.

Oh, shit, Faro said silently.

Now there was nothing to do but wait for Pop Smol-lett.

When he came in, Faro had no doubt of who it was. The tall but stooped frame, the rags that clothed him, and the filthy, matted hair and beard could have been the attributes of any number of Louse Pointers, from what he had seen; but only the man the attackers had described would have sported the expression of lunatic glee and malice that shone on this old man's face.

The keen eight-inch knife blade jutting from his fist helped clinch the identification.

The apparition cackled and shuffled toward him. "Hey, hey," he whispered happily. "What's this, then? A tasty, plump fowl, all nicely trussed up, is it, ready for poor old Pop's dinner, yes? Now, do we disjoint him first and gut him after, or is it the other way 'round? No matter, no matter, anything'll do for a start."

Faro drummed his heels frantically on the stone floor as the old horror approached him, then subsided and closed his eyes as the knife descended slowly toward him.

He flinched at a sudden pressure at—unexpectedly —the coil of rope at his wrists. Then, to his astonishment, it fell away, and his arms were free. His eyes snapped open and he sat bolt upright.

Pop Smollett was behind him now. Faro winced at a knife prick at the back of his neck; then the gag was cut away. The old man moved in front of him and stared down at him gravely. "It grieves me to see you in such low company, my boy," he said. "Those three are no fit associates for an honest young gambler."

His features, no longer maniacally twisted, were calm—and, under the straggle of beard, finally recognizable.

"Holy shit," Faro said. "Doc!"

The old man bowed. "Jackson Lafitte Prentiss at your service, young Faro."

Chapter 10

Faro was understandably surprised to see that the man he had accepted as his destined murderer was Doc Prentiss, known through the states and territories as one of the most adept swindlers the Union had ever produced—and, more cogently, the friend and companion of Faro's father, A. B. Burr, and the intermittent but effective tutor of the youthful Faro himself in the old riverboat days.

"What are you doing here, Doc?" Faro asked.

"Cutting your feet loose so you can use them to make tracks out of here right away," the old confidence man muttered. "It would interest me strangely to know the reason for your own presence in this hellhole, but I have the good sense to save the social conversation for more restful circumstances. That precious crew went out the front way—we'll take the back, with our fingers crossed, taking care to move as silently as the wily Indian."

Outside, they slipped furtively down the dark street. "You came here tonight from San Bernardo, I expect," Doc said in a low voice.

"Yeah."

"How?"

"Drifted down in a bitty sailboat."

"Damn. I'd hoped you'd ridden in—in a pinch your horse could carry us both. A boat's no good to us—even if we knew how to handle sail, which I doubt, we'd be too good a target out in the river, with the moon still that much up."

"Could we maybe steal a horse or so?" Faro asked, padding along beside Doc as silently as he could manage.

Doc grunted sourly. "Every third man here was stealing horses before he'd left off sucking tit. Those that have mounts make sure they keep 'em. The kind of precautions they take'd be eye-openers to lawmen and Pinkertons. Ahorse and afloat are out, so it's afoot for you and me, young Faro. There's a pretty fair river trail to San Bernardo, and it's not above ten miles off."

"We could walk it in maybe two hours," Faro said.

"And trot it in less, which is what I'd advise. Nolan made it pretty clear that what he wanted you left as was a Pop Smollett special, which means that if he or Rick or Fred take a look in there and don't find blood ten feet up on the walls, they'll figure I've played them false and start looking for us."

The last decaying building of Louse Point was behind them now, and they were jogging along a sandy track that wound between scrub masking the river on their left and a screen of twisted trees on their right.

Faro tried to adjust the rhythm of his speech to his jolting gait. "What is this Pop Smollett stuff? Way you look, and what those fellows said of you, this Smollett

116

is about as low as you can get without being put in a zoo. My recollection, whether you was doing the green goods, the gold bricks, the electric belts, the wire game, or only traveling in snake oil, you set store by being well turned-out and gentlemanly in all your ways and appearances."

"Because I was separating the marks from their money, young Faro. Now, come down to it, the man that gets money is the man that looks as if money *belongs* to him—as if any loose greenbacks that the mark happens to have in his pocket are there by mistake, and are the rightful property of the man that has the look of owning it. You have that kind of bearing, and the details of the scam hardly matter, for a mark with a proper sense of his place in the scheme of things'll be glad of any reasonable excuse to pass over the spondulicks, and just hope you don't charge him interest for having kept hold of it for so long."

Doc took a few puffing breaths and resumed his discourse. "But information, that's another matter. To get *information,* you got to look as if you had never heard of it, you wouldn't know what it was if it bit you, and you wouldn't have the wits to remember any of it if you heard it. Down there in Louse Point, fellows that'd reach for their shooters if asked the time of day by anything that looked like a man and brother, those same fellows would unburden themselves of the most dangerous stuff you can imagine, and care no more than a fart in the wind if they were overheard by a crazy old mule-turd like Pop Smollett. And yes, I will tell you, with my predispositions and attributes, it was no fun turning myself into that walking maggot-heap. But I did learn something from it, even at my age— it's wonderful, and saddening, how easy it is to get a reputation for being completely and beyond-redemption loathsome. I hadn't but to do my act a little and start some stories going around, and I was set. The worst of men would talk as freely around me as though they were in the privy."

"What was the information you was after?" Faro said, the words jolted out of him by his stride.

"Well, mainly how to get out of there once I was in," Doc said.

"You are doing that now, ain't you?"

"There is a matter of freightage involved. It was in my mind to take something with me that I couldn't carry on my own, and anything in the way of bulky and noticeable leaving Louse Point attracts attentions of the kind I wouldn't welcome. Nor, come right down to it, survive, probably."

Faro jogged on, saying nothing.

"My narrative doesn't pique your interest?" Doc panted.

"If you got the wind left to go at this all round about, even whilst you're running, thass fine with me," Faro said. "But I don't intend to spend my own breath helping you spin it out."

"Well, fair enough. It's in my bones to put the best face on a story at all times, just so as not to get rusty when coming up against the marks. But all the same, I have to come at this kind of slaunchwise, if it's to make sense. You see, when I was a younger man by a little more than half, I spent some time down around here. Was still a journeyman grifter then, though well past the 'prentice stage, and doing well at it, even though the Mexican War was coming on, pursuing my accustomed course of taking from the rich and giving to the poor—for it was the normal course of things that I'd be lower in pocket than the man I was bilking —and—"

"Like that Robin Hood man you told me of," Faro said flatly.

"Some," Doc said. "Now, funny you should mention that, because—"

"You was operating under that Hood's right monicker, Locksley."

Doc broke stride and stared at Faro. "Now, how the hell—"

Faro, who had also stopped, glared at him in exasperation. "Lemme tell you what you—shit!" He flung himself to the ground and laid his ear against it, urgently waving Doc to silence. The old man nodded, crouched, and pressed his own head to the earth. "Hoofbeats," he murmured.

"For sure."

"Pursuit."

"Not likely a excursion to be first in line for the Catamount's breakfast," Faro said. He glanced to the left. The brush there was sparse, and, if spotted there, they would be flushed onto the sandbanks bordering the river, clearly seen moving targets in the moonlight. Not moving for very long, likely. He grabbed Doc's arm and urged him silently toward the gnarled trees to the right of the track.

The slanting finger of a crownless dead tree, bone-white in the moonlight, gave him a sudden inspiration; he leaped for it, hauled, felt and heard the crack as it gave and toppled to lie across the path at an angle. It formed a nearly invisible barrier over the shadowed trail perhaps eight feet from the ground.

"I partly divine your intention," Doc whispered dolefully, "and I don't like it. They'd have ridden right past."

"And then on back. We got to use this trail, and they know it. We take to the woods, we'll likely wander

119

forever. The one thing I learned from the damn war *I* was in was that if you're going to have a fight, you'd best pick the ground."

In a few moments, as they crouched behind the gnarled trees, they heard the sound of hoofbeats. They became louder, and then the dim shape of a horse and rider came into view.

With a solid thumping sound and a howl, the shape's human component was detached from its equine and deposited on the trail.

"What the hell happened?" The fallen man's companion came up and peered down from his mount.

"Run into a damn tree in this patch of dark here."

"Noticed it was leanin' when I rode by yestiddy."

"Well, it's leaned all the damn way over now. Listen, we'd of caught 'em up by now if they was walkin'. I say they cut into the woods somewheres a way back, or else cut out downriver."

"If they done that last, Nolan'll be on 'em soon. My say is they could be ahead of us still, had they decided to run it, which in their shoes I'd incline to. Whyn't you cast back alongst the trail and see if you can pick up any sign they took to the woods—I'll go on a mile or so and see if I spot 'em ahead. Easy enough to bring 'em down with the rifle, soon's ever I do. If I don't see 'em by the time I've got as far as they could of run, I'll come back and help you check out the woods. Fair?"

"Enough."

The second man edged his mount past his companion and disappeared up the trail, ducking to avoid the leaning tree.

The man seated on the ground stood and approached his horse. "I can take him just as he's mounting," Faro whispered. "Be ready with that toad-sticker in case I run into trouble." Doc nodded.

Faro slipped from the trees, padded swiftly across the trail and caught the man just as he had set one foot in the stirrup and tensed to heave his other leg over the saddle. Reid's knuckleduster-pistol nestled in his palm took the man neatly just behind the right ear with a satisfyingly solid impact, and he dropped without a sound.

Doc emerged from cover and joined Faro in staring down at his victim. Faro found a coil of rope dangling from the saddle and secured his hands and legs, then wadded the man's own kerchief in his slack mouth.

"Help me drag him into the woods."

Doc gestured with his knife. "Wouldn't it be safer . . . ?"

"What for? Mainest thing they're after is to keep what happened back there hushed up—he ain't about to raise the alarm after us even after he wakes up and gets loose. Besides, by then we'll be long gone."

"I guess I've been Pop Smollett too long," Doc sighed. "Not that Rick'd be any loss. Done two spite killings in Louse Point that I know of, and God knows what before he got there. The one that went on ahead is Fred, by the way. He's worse."

"This'll improve him some, then," Faro said, hefting the stubby pistol.

It was fifteen minutes later that Fred, returning down the trail, stopped at the sight of Rick's horse, standing with dropped reins. "Rick? Where the hell—"

Doc, crouched in a patch of brush, called hoarsely in his best approximation of the unconscious man's voice: "Fred! Over here—tracks goin' down t' the river!"

"The shit you say! What would they do that for?"

Fred dismounted and ran for the brushy side of the trail. As he pawed his way through the sparse growth, Faro rose almost from beneath his feet and laid the knuckleduster deftly at the base of his skull—then cursed as it rebounded from a mat of greasy hair without doing any more than sending the outlaw staggering, and pawing for the gun at his waist.

Faro sprang for him, and then at the midpoint of his lunge twisted aside, as Fred brought up his pistol and slammed off a shot at him. His boot slid in the sandy soil and he hit the ground heavily, the impact sending the Reid's skittering out of his hand.

Fred stood six feet away, the gun leveled at Faro. "Head shot for quick an' easy, or one in the balls, for slow an' painful, your choice—quick, tell me where Pop Smollett's at!"

"Right *here,* Freddie boy," Doc crooned with an eerie chuckle, seemingly materializing out of the darkness to crook an arm across Fred's throat and lay his knifepoint against the lowest button of Fred's shirt. "Old Pop's here and ready for work, yes he is. Oh, one move, one *twitch,* and *in* she goes, and then *up* so far's your breastbone, and all your pretty insides spread out."

Fred stood very still and let his gun drop. Faro scooped it up.

"That was pretty convincing, the Pop Smollett act," Faro said a few minutes later. They were riding up the trail, having left Fred knocked out and tied up beside his colleague.

"Convincing's my stock in trade," Doc said. "For a man who can with equal facility portray Colonel Humphrey Rowayton, Chief Spotted Tail, and a hellfire preacher, being a criminal lunatic is child's play."

"Not to mention being one Locksley," Faro said. "Would you mind giving me the details of that one, as you was doing before we stopped to entertain Fred and Rick?"

Much of Doc's story paralleled what Faro had heard from Marshal Pratt: the plan to assault the Mexican fort and waylay the pay train, the fight, the retreat to the river. Where the accounts diverged was at the end.

"When the Mexicans hit the boat and holed it and it started to fill and sink, a splinter took me in the scalp and I bled like a stuck pig—must have looked as if I was killed on the spot. The other fellows struck out for the American shore, but I stuck with the boat 'til it sank. It was still near the Mexican side, and shallow, and I hated like fury to let that chest get away from me, so long as there was any chance of keeping hold of it. When it finally grounded, it was only about six feet under the water. I shucked my shirt and dove and tied it to one of the handles on the chest for a marker, then swam ashore on the Mexican side and hid up for a few days 'til the troops left. They pulled the fort garrison out with them, as they were needed where the fighting was, so the place was deserted. I humped the chest ashore and buried it under the flagstones of the fort, figuring I'd come back some time with a couple of pack mules and make off with it—sharing out, of course, with McGree and Holabird."

"Of course," Faro said. "Now, that was thirty-some years ago. How come you ain't found the occasion to cash in before now?"

"Well, right after the war, when things settled down a bit, I came down to Mexico, with the idea that I'd study out the situation and find the right time to get up here and get the gold without attracting undue atten-

tion. But it happened in the course of—ah, business—
that I chanced to offend an important official."

"Who?"

"Santa Anna. It was a lesson to me never to skin a
mark who has been made supreme dictator of the
country I'm working in, not that the question comes
up that often." Doc, it developed, had persuaded the
Mexican potentate to invest in a plantation of chicle
trees he had acquired cheaply—"invest" meaning
paying out something like ten times the price Doc had
—with the idea of marketing their sap as a replace-
ment for chewing tobacco. When Santa Anna realized
the inherent folly of this notion, his vengefulness knew
no bounds, and Doc was obliged to leave Mexico in
haste.

"Even after they threw him out, the place was too
hot for me," Doc said. "He had got me down in the
books as a murderer, robber, coiner, child molester,
revolutionary, oppressor of the poor, and dealer in
substandard chili peppers. Anything that anybody
that ever came to power in Mexico could conceivably
abominate, why, Santa Anna had convicted me of and
sent out my engraving and description to every post of
police, *rurales* or *federales*. Friends who have passed
through tell me that about every lawman in Mexico
has dreams of shooting me on sight. So, even for all
that money, I deemed it imprudent to cross the border."

But then, some time back, the news had come to
him that the border had changed—that the fort where
he had buried the treasure was now, if not statutorily
in America, at least out of Mexico.

"So I assumed the Pop Smollett identity and came
to Louse Point to spy out the land. And I tell you, I
almost wish I'd taken my chances when it was in Mex-

ico. Pop Smollett, the crazy old degenerate, why, he
fit in just fine at Louse Point—but Pop Smollett, looking for the hire of a pack mule and carrying something
of interest out of town, that'd be something else. Those
cutthroats would have had my money and my life,
quick as winking, if they'd had any suspicion I had
any."

Doc had spent several weeks in Louse Point, trying
to work out a safe way to retrieve his proceeds from
that long-ago battle, to no effect. And then, to his astonishment, he found himself invited to make away
with the son of his old friend A. B. Burr.

"Which brings us, young Faro, to the matter of *your*
presence in that pesthole—and, indeed, in this part of
the country. Will you oblige me?"

Faro did so, touching on how Reid had euchred him
into coming to San Bernardo, coerced him into coop-
erating—"The Santa Anna method," Doc commented,
"I can tell you, it's effective"—and assigned him to
shadowing Jim McGree, thus finally bringing him to
Louse Point.

"Which it is clear that it's meaningful that Jim Mc-
Gree and Bob Holabird has dealings together," Faro
concluded, "but I can't puzzle out what that meaning
is."

"As I told you, young Faro, the man that seems to
be going after information finds it hard to come by,
but the man that looks as if he wouldn't know it from
buffalo chips gets it showered on him. Puzzle no further. I have the answer, and shall now impart it."

In the pre-dawn light, the streets of San Bernardo
were deserted, or almost. Faro and Doc, having abandoned their borrowed horses a few hundred yards

from town, peered from behind a shed at a stocky figure walking up the main street from the river.

"Jim McGree," Faro muttered. "Must of made good time sailing upriver."

"Time-consuming," Doc said, "but a damn good way of avoiding any troublesome questions asked about hiring a horse. Let him get to the Catamount, and then we'll go wake that marshal up."

Marshal Pratt was not well pleased at being awakened by Faro's urgent rapping at the door of his quarters behind his office, but responded to the urgency of his request for a conference, and took a dour satisfaction at rousing Reid at the campsite the Ranger had chosen at the edge of town and fetching him in.

Faro, Doc, and Pratt sipped at steaming mugs of coffee the marshal had prepared. Reid declined in favor of a pre-breakfast dose of his tonic, on the grounds that caffeine was an unnatural and deleterious substance.

"That Sachem Onondaga stuff is cheap goods," Doc muttered to Faro. "I could get him a good case price on Chief Tonto's Silver Remedy, that packs a lot more wallop."

"He is walloped enough now, Doc," Faro confided. "Let's see this thing through without experimenting on him."

"Let me get the straight of it," Pratt said. "You are telling us that Jim McGree and Bob Holabird have agreed betwixt 'em to fire up this feud—seen to all the doings that's so far been done—with the notion of destroying both their families?"

"It was Louse Point that gave them the idea," Doc said. "Now, that's just a little boil on the behind of the

State of Texas, and just serves as a kind of rest home for hardcases, as the law doesn't run there. But suppose there was a big area that had no law to it—a kind of bandit kingdom, you might call it—where there was no effective law at all. And suppose that was right here, in and around San Bernardo. It could serve as a stronghold from which raids could be made into New Mexico, Mexico itself, other parts of Texas. This is a remote area, that nobody much cares about who doesn't live here, and it wouldn't be that hard to seize control of it. By the time it was clear what had happened, it'd take the Army to dislodge the men who'd done that, and the chances are, the way things go in Washington now, that there'd be some compromise made that would leave Jim and Bob running their own private fief, or maybe a new state. We all recall a time when there wasn't a West Virginia—is a West Texas so out of the question? And the only thing that really stands in their way is that Alex McGree and Mal Holabird, whatever differences they may have over that business of the Mexican treasure—" here Doc glared at Faro, who had failed to muffle a snort of laughter "—have cooperated to maintain law and order in this region. If the influence of the Holabirds and McGrees is broken, there will be chaos here, and it's Jim and Bob who'll profit. Very shrewdly, they've decided to let Alex McGree and Mal Holabird do most of the work, by stirring up the old trouble between them."

Jim and Bob, wandering hardcases, had met in the Indian Territory, Doc explained, and, discovering their common connections with the major families of the San Bernardo area, had devised their plan. Bob had returned to claim the fatted calf of the reformed prodigal from his father—in his case, the post of purchasing agent for Mal Holabird's enterprises—and Jim had turned up with bona-fide credentials as a moderately remote cousin. They had by now contrived to dominate the Louse Point community, and were readying it to participate in the all-out war between the Holabirds and the McGrees which they were fomenting.

"When that's over," Doc said, "the idea is that the one surviving Holabird and the one surviving McGree will repent and make peace—and, since that will be Jim and Bob, take over. The thing is, there's not much time. I haven't heard any clear talk, but I get the feeling that there's something big coming along soon, something frightful enough done to one side or the other so that there'll be no stopping the war."

"Then we've got to move fast," Reid said.

"For sure," Pratt agreed. "But move how, that's the question."

"Get Mal Holabird and Alex McGree to drop this feud and unite against—"

"The one of 'em's son and the other of 'em's long-lost cousin, *sure*. I have knowed those two, Captain Reid, for more years than you can shake a donkey at, and I will tell you, they are notional and hardheaded. It would take some tall convincing to get 'em to see that, I want you to know. That's one problem we got on our plate. Another one," he said, turning to Doc, "is just where you come in. What I know of you is that you come from Louse Point, which is *no* recommendation, that you're vouched for as reliable by Mr. Blake, which is *some,* and that he's vouched for by Captain Reid, who is vouched for by the State of Texas, and all that is stretching the vouchings a little thin."

"I think your two problems might cancel each other out, Marshal," Doc assured him. "What you need to make these two old mustangs see the light of sweet

128

reason, is a professional persuader, a man that can make the better cause seem the worse, black seem white, or what you choose. And where but in that thieves' kitchen would you find in this fair and law-abiding territory one of the nation's ace confidence men taking up temporary residence? Mr. Blake here will assure you that Jackson Lafitte Prentiss has no superiors and damn few peers in the arts of larceny by fraud, guile, and barefaced swindling. And there is no reason that talent can't be employed in the service of the public good instead of private enrichment. Show me this Holabird and that McGree, and I'll have them ready to disown their scapegrace kin in a trice."

"Is this old coot telling us the truth?" Reid asked.

Faro nodded. "Doc could sell you sand for salt, and have you place another order next time he come round," he said.

"Being but a small-town lawman, it's new to me to have a man recommend hisself to me on the grounds that he's a prime-grade crook," Pratt said heavily. "But seeing that you, Reid, is what the Rangers sent me, and that Blake is what you drug in, I don't know that I got any reason to draw lines any more. One thing I would admire to know, though," he added, turning to Doc, "is why you was temporary residencing at Louse Point. Wouldn't think there was much pickings there for a confidence man."

Faro watched Doc with interest, quickly calculating the odds against his giving the true reason for his sojourn in the outlaw hangout. Nine-nine-nine repeating to one, was how it struck him.

Doc coughed delicately. "Not to mince words, gentlemen, a man traveling in my line of work has what you might call opportunities, and I confess that I've availed myself of them. When there were adverse judgments brought against me in the courts of five states and three territories hereabouts, I deemed it advisable to retire to the limbo afforded by the uncertain legal status of Louse Point."

"What kind of judgments?" Pratt asked.

"In paternity suits," Doc said with simple pride.

Chapter 11

"There is one thing, Doc," Faro said, watching his friend adjust his cravat knot in Faro's room at the Catamount. "Now that we have got you washed and shaved at the barber, and fitted you out in them duds from the dry-goods, you don't look like Pop Smollett no more—"

"A mask I am glad to doff, my boy," Doc said, stepping back from the mirror over the chest of drawers.

"—but what do you do when you drop in on Holabird, and he takes one look and says, 'My old friend Bob Locksley, back from the dead!'?"

"Locksley was thirty years younger, twenty pounds stouter, decked out in an Imperial beard and a moustache that turned up at the ends, and affected a remarkably offensive military swagger. In any case, he won't be *expecting* to see Locksley, so he won't be searching out the one or two clues that might give me away. Don't worry about that."

"If you say so." Faro followed Doc out of the room, past Jim McGree's still-closed door, and downstairs to the charred eggs that the Catamount offered for breakfast.

Reid was waiting for them. "I begin to believe this could work," he said, looking at Doc. "That is considerable of a transformation."

"Consider it a revelation, Captain," Doc said. "I have shed a husk and emerged, quivering in the light of day, to try my wings."

When Doc left the ground, it was not by means of wings, but by throwing one leg across the windowsill of Mal Holabird's office at the rear of his store, and stepping inside.

"You start off getting the mark alarmed and sputtering," he had told Faro, "and then show that you mean him no harm, why, that's the first step toward making him putty in your hands."

Alarmed and sputtering Mal Holabird indeed seemed to be to Faro and Reid, who now stood against the back wall of Holabird's office and craned their ears to overhear what was going on inside.

"Bob Holabird about?" Doc said.

They heard Mal's reply: "What the thunderation! No, he ain't, and you can just jackknife yourself out of here fast's you come in, or you'll get the drubbing of your life!"

"No need for drubbing to come into it," Doc said. "If Bob's not here, my good man, why don't you just fetch me Old Mallet?"

"Old Mallet?" Holabird said bewilderedly.

"Bob's affectionate term for his father and your employer," Doc said. "I expect you clerks don't feel comfortable using family nicknames."

132

"Firstly, I am no clerk, and secondly, any man that names me mallet is asking to get one of that article laid about his ears. I am Malcolm Holabird, owner and sole proprietor of this and most other places of business hereabouts, and I would be obliged if you would tell me why you have leaped into my office window, and before the opening of business hours at that, with this load of nonsense."

"Mr. Holabird, sir! A pleasure to meet you—I am always happier dealing with principals, anyhow. I am Geronimo."

"That you ain't," Holabird said flatly. "I saw him once, and he is shorter, and of the Indian persuasion."

"That's the name Bob and I fixed on that I should use in my dealings with your company, man," Doc said urgently. "He picked it—a pretty notion—because of that lot of French Foreign Legion rifles I brought in from Mexico and you sold to the Apaches. I haven't come here about that, but now that it's come up, I'd appreciate something on account for that deal —it's been a couple of months now."

"Rifles to the 'Paches?" Holabird said faintly.

"Like coals to Newcastle, I agree," Doc said, "but if they'll pay out for what you sell them, why worry? What I am really here about is the shipment that's due in tonight."

"Shipment?"

"I can understand you don't want to talk of it aloud. Even in our trade, there are things that don't sit so easily, and all I can say is that the goods might be dirty, but the money isn't, Old Mallet. But if Bob's not here, I know I can rely on you to handle it—where is he, by the way?"

"Rode out to call on some of the trading posts we supply," Mal said weakly.

Doc guffawed. "You and he share the same taste in jokes, don't you, Old Mallet? 'Trading posts'! Well, we both know what *that* means, eh? Now, the shipment's coming in at the usual place, and at the time Bob and I set. That's really all I came to say. But I'll add that I'm glad you're taking a hand in it yourself—as I said, it's always better to deal with principals. Good morning to you, sir."

Faro and Reid saw Doc step down from the building's rear window, and joined him in a frantic run that took them around a corner before Mal Holabird could collect himself enough to peer out.

"I heard every word of that," Reid said, "and I couldn't make any sense of it."

"There wasn't any in it," Doc said. "All I did was brush in some colors and leave it to Mal's imagination to draw the outlines. What he'll make of that *shipment* business, I have no idea—I made it sound filthy, so he'll have to decide whether I was talking about prime-grade opium or kidnapped whores. Main thing is, right now he'll be calling in Bob's books and checking them, and sending to see if he's actually gone out to those trading posts. I have broken his trust in Bob, and got him to considering that the lad might be playing him false—chiefly by never suggesting such a thing, but letting him leap to that conclusion himself. I rather liked the 'Old Mallet' touch—that would be bound to goad him."

"So now?" Reid said.

"Give him time to get in a stew. I'll wager that the books won't parse as they should, and it's a certainty that no trading post will have heard of Bob lately, as he's known to us to be in Louse Point. When you come in, say about noon, display your Ranger commission, and explain what Bob's up to to him, he'll be ready for you."

"I'll allow that," Reid said. "What's your plan for convincing Alex McGree that Jim's the same sort of low-life?"

Doc considered for a moment. "I think this might be a task for Faro, here. You retain all your skills, my boy? You can still deal from the bottom, top or mid-deck, as you choose, force a card, manipulate the holdout?"

With an uneasy glance at the Ranger captain, Faro said, "Well, yeah, I expect, so long as it was in a good cause."

"The best," Doc said. "Captain Reid, you have to work into this as well. Let me lay it out for you."

"It gravels me to go back to the Lazy M without better news for Cousin Alex," Jim McGree said. He flicked his whip lightly over the backs of the team drawing the buckboard.

"No cooks for hire?" Faro asked.

"Four no's come in by wire, four others not heard from," Jim said. "I left two dollars with the telegraph clerk to give to someone that would ride out with any answers that come in later."

"Good thinking," Faro said. Five minutes before joining Jim for the journey back to the ranch, he had dropped in at the Western Union office and learned that the line had not yet been repaired.

"Was word of a spread north and west of here, I heard it in town, that has a hand that worked oncet as a trail cook," Jim said. "Was in my mind, I'd let Cousin Alex know how things stand, then ride out there and see about that."

"A credit to you, how you look after his interests,"

Faro said, quickly concluding that Jim McGree's ride would be to the south and east—to Louse Point, for a final conference with Bob Holabird before whatever balloon they were inflating went up.

"I will be glad to play a few hands with you," Alex McGree said, the glumness of his tone belying his words. "If I'm lucky at cards, at least that'll be something—there ain't much in that line else happening to me. Wasn't for Jim, I declare I don't know what I'd do. That boy, distant kin though he is, is busting his butt to keep the Lazy M going and stand off Mal Holabird and his crew."

Faro consulted his watch. According to the plan Doc had outlined and he and Reid had agreed to, the Ranger would be showing up in about ten minutes—just right.

Ten minutes later, Alex McGree was saying, "It's wonderful lucky we wasn't playing for money, Sam, else I'd of been wiped out for fair. Each time, I had what looked like a sure winning hand, and each time, you just edged me out."

"That's how the cards fall, Cousin Alex," Faro said.

The McGree hired girl entered the parlor. "Mr. Alex. A man on the porch, says he's a Texas Ranger."

Alex McGree rose to inspect the new arrival, and Faro followed him from the parlor.

"Mr. McGree? Captain John Reid, Texas Rangers. Appreciate it if you would inspect my commission before we talk—I want you to be confident in your mind that I'm what I claim to be."

"Don't need that, Captain—Alex McGree can size up a man at first sight, and no questions. I make an exception in the case of one Mal Holabird, in whom I

136

was mistook—something tells me that you are maybe here about the trouble 'twixt him and me?"

As Faro stood back, listening to this conversation, he heard a rustle behind him and turned to see, looking wide-eyed at the Ranger, Dora McGree. Fuck the luck, he said inwardly—two people on this whole damn ranch saw the man that was supposed to be roughing me up on behalf of the Holabirds, and one of 'em has to come along just now!

"Sam," Dora said shrilly, "isn't that—"

She stopped speaking as Faro, desperate to cut off her revelation, reached out and grabbed one breast, squeezing it hard but not, he hoped, painfully.

She glared at him. "Cousin Sam Jenkins," she whispered fiercely, "I could knee you so as to geld you, right here and now, and you better tell me why I shouldn't."

"Wanted to attract your attention," Faro muttered. "Was that, or clap my hand acrost your mouth, and likely set you to screaming. Seemed to me what I done, you'd deal with more private, like. But I apologize."

"I accept," she whispered. "Now, you want to take your hand off?"

"Oh, yeah." He withdrew his hand, registering that the nipple had stiffened under his palm as if impelled by a spring.

He wondered what kind of lie he could improvise to keep her from creating a fuss that would shatter the plan Doc had worked up, decided that there was none, and plunged ahead: "That man's a Texas Ranger, I ain't your cousin, and him and me are here to stop the feud and sink Bob Holabird and Jim McGree up to their eyeballs in sheep-dip, and it'd pleasure me a good deal if you would keep mum and let us get at it, and

137

if you go off like a steam whistle, the whole damn thing will fall apart, so would you for Christ's sake keep quiet?"

She looked at him thoughtfully. "You're telling me Jim's a rotten apple?"

"Soft to the core," Faro assured her.

"That's what makes me credit the rest. Being around him makes me feel as if I was being crawled on by spiders, and it sickened me that Grandpa took to him so. Get on with what you mean to, then."

She moved away from him, then looked back over her shoulder, her left hand resting on her bosom as Faro's had a moment before. "You were asking where my room was, yesterday—if you really want to know, it's second from the left of the staircase."

She vanished up the stairs, and Faro turned to where Reid, tall hat twisted in his hands, was continuing his conversation with Alex McGree.

"—important I talk to you. Touches on your cousin Jim."

"As I heard it, you come here to tell me how you meant to deal with the iniquities of Mal Holabird and Bob Holabird and all them, so I don't see what Jim, that is my mainstay and chiefest support, has to do with it. But come on into the parlor. You too, Sam —I believe we can play a hand or so of poker whilst I'm listening to the captain, without missing too much of what he has to say."

"What do you know about Jim?" Reid said, when they were seated, Alex McGree and Faro at a small round oak table, Reid on a plush sofa against the wall.

"That he is kin and that I knowed him at first sight for a man I could take to," Alex McGree said. "Like Cousin Sam Jenkins here."

Faro dealt five cards, face down.

"What do you know about what he did and where he was before he came out here?"

Alex McGree picked up his cards and studied them, his face tightening as—as Faro read it—he attempted to suppress an expression of glee. "What I care to, which is nothing. How a man deals with me is what counts with me; I don't go poking and prying into what he may of done before we met up."

"Putting it as a maybe, suppose I was to tell you that Jim is an out-and-out thief, and that he's in cahoots with Bob Holabird to wreck you and Mal Holabird both, by turning that old trouble between you into a full-blown feud?"

Alex McGree stiffened and glared at the Ranger, then, looking once more at his cards, relaxed. "I am glad you have put it as a maybe, and so ain't said any such thing. If you had done so, it'd of been my duty and pleasure to go for your windpipe and eyeballs with my thumbs, with Cousin Sam standing by to see fair play. As it is, I will pretend to deafness. The Rangers ain't what they were in Big Foot Wallace's time, going by you, Captain."

"You know Wallace?" At McGree's curt nod, Reid continued, "He ever tell you about the time he was chasing those Indians that run off his horses, and when he was closing in on them, he dumped about a bushel of nuts down inside his shirt to serve him as armor?"

"And they shot arrer after arrer into him until he was like as a porcupine, only all the arrers stuck amongst the nuts, so as he wasn't hurt, and the Indians took fright and run off—accourse I know about that, and from Big Foot's own lips," Alex McGree said. He looked again at his cards and told Faro, "I believe I will stand pat."

"Last year, Wallace told me that was the best yarn

he ever made up," Reid said. "What pleasured him most was how them that heard it kept a straight face, as if they actually believed it."

"Hit you with how many?" Faro said.

"I told you, I'm standing pat!" Alex McGree split his glare equally between Reid and Faro.

"Wrong play, Cousin Alex," Faro said coldly. "You are telling me by that that you've got a hand you can't improve, a straight, a flush, a full house or so. And I doubt that."

"As it ain't for money, I don't mind telling you that you are right and wrong at the same time, Sam," Alex McGree said. "I ain't got any of what you mentioned, yet I couldn't improve it on any draw. You want to work out that riddle?"

"Don't have to," Faro said. "Draw one and see." With a puzzled look at him, McGree withdrew one card from his hand and picked up the one Faro had dealt him. Without looking at it, he displayed the remaining four. "Cousin, you want to tell me how I'd of improved four kings?"

"Take a look," Faro said. McGree turned over the last card he had been dealt. "What in . . . ?"

It was the king of spades.

"So you improved your hand by the luck of the draw," Faro said flatly.

"Five kings?" McGree said wonderingly.

"But not a winning hand," Faro said, exposing his own five aces.

McGree sat for a moment, silent and shaken. "Sam," he said, "what are you—"

"For openers, I'm not Sam, nor yet no Jenkins," Faro said. "I shoved that lie down your throat, and you took it. And, this evening, I dealt you what I wanted to and myself what I wanted to, and took every hand, and you put it down to how the cards fell. And right now I rang a extra king and a extra ace in the game under your nose, and you none the wiser. So you can work out for yourself what your judging of a man by how he seems to you is worth. Are you maybe ready to hear what Captain Reid's got to say about Jim? And how to save your ass and the Lazy M's?"

"Well, I will say it is a relief to me," Alex McGree said, half an hour later. "I don't hold it that much against Mal Holabird that he done me out of my share of that Mex gold in '45, but it grieved me that he'd turn so spiteful as to try to ruin me. So it was Jim and his Bob that was behind all this that's been happening lately? And that old buzzard is willing to admit it?"

"I had a talk with him this forenoon," Reid said. "After he had had some information from . . . ah, other sources, and had checked over Bob's books and where he had been when he was supposed to have been where he wasn't, so to speak. Yes, he has now accepted that Bob is a bad hat and a fomenter of needless trouble, and he's willing—anxious, even—to meet with you, tonight, if you can manage it, to work out what to do about stopping Jim and Bob."

"It ain't much but the shank of the evening," Alex McGree said after a while. "And maybe a ride into town would ginger me up some. He wants to talk with me, Mal Holabird can damned well give me a bed for the night to boot."

After Reid's and McGree's departure for San Bernardo, Faro set out a game of solitaire on the table in the parlor, and began playing it out.

Diamond three on spade four.

No way to get this story into a shape a young woman like her could understand . . .

Spade eight on heart nine.

Best face I can put on it, I've criminalized her cousin, showed myself a liar and false-pretenser, and set something going that nobody can see the end of, except that it works out to trouble for the Lazy M. . . .

A lone ace, for another whole goddam pile to start up.

So just steer clear of her, no messes. Any girl's tit would of snapped up like that, given the shock and startlement. . . .

A one-eyed jack twitched as it slid to cover a staring, smiling queen.

Faro rose and slid the cards together with the game uncompleted, gave them a fast shuffle, and set them down in a neatly squared deck.

Second from the left off the staircase, she'd said.

Chapter 12

"Looking at it one way," Reid said, "my job is done. I got Mr. Holabird and Mr. McGree together last night, and they agreed that there wasn't a feud between them, and never had been. And the settling of that feud is what I was sent here to do and, with the help of Mr. Blake and Dr. Prentiss, have done. Not to mention Marshal Pratt."

"Which you didn't," Pratt said, "as far as I could make out." He, Alex McGree, Doc, and Faro watched the Ranger captain as he stared back at them broodingly, leaning against the wall of the marshal's office. Mal Holabird divided his attention between Reid and Doc, whom he eyed doubtfully. Reid and Pratt had conspired to persuade him that "Geronimo" was actually a special operative of the Rangers—which McGree had also been told—but the memory of the deception that had led him to accept the fact of his son's perfidy still appeared to rankle.

"Jim McGree's and Bob Holabird's plans to set the principal men of this area at each other's throats have come to nothing," Reid went on.

"Jim sets foot on the Lazy M again, he will leave it drug at a rope's end behind a fast horse until the horse founders, the rope breaks, or he is wore to a nub," Alex McGree said.

"I have cut Bob off of my payroll and out of my will," Mal Holabird said.

"But what made those plans possible is still there," Reid said. "The outlaw sanctuary of Louse Point."

"Which not you nor I, nor up to Rutherford B. Hayes has the right to set foot in bearing warrants nor with the intention to pursue and arrest," Pratt pointed out, "it not being part of the State of Texas or the U. S. of A."

Doc tipped back in his chair, his hand jammed into his trouser pockets, and surveyed the ceiling thoughtfully. "I take it, Captain, that it cuts you to the quick to fulfill the letter of your assignment, even as notably as you have done, yet leave the spirit of it unmet?"

Reid nodded somberly.

"The Louse Point community will remain a toxic reservoir, poisoning the area with its criminal influence?"

"Bound to," Reid said.

"Yet, the law reading as it does, there is not a damned thing you can do about it?"

Reid nodded. Pratt, McGree, and Holabird looked glum.

"Well, then, man," Doc said, "let's break the law!"

He overrode the flurry of comment that followed this pronouncement: "What makes Louse Point the Louse Point it is is the fact of settlement by the citizens of our neighbor republic to the south—the houses, fort, and so on. Now, if there was nothing there but a barren sandspit, if not a stone remained upon a stone or a timber nailed to a timber, who then could say where Louse Point was or had ever been? If we raze the place to the ground and sow it with salt, we're done with it. Louse Point *delenda est*."

"The Louse Pointers might have something to say about that," Faro said.

"Mr. McGree and Mr. Holabird have a few score stout fellows at their beck," Doc replied. "If we proceed with daring and resolution, we can kick everybody's ass the hell out of there."

Reid walked over to Doc and looked down at him thoughtfully. "Sir, I am proud to know you," he said after a moment. "You are thinking like a Ranger."

"What do you think of our flotilla?" Doc asked. A day after the conference in the marshal's office, he and Faro were walking by the river, observing the hasty but efficient assembly of a dozen huge log rafts by a crew composed of Mal Holabird's employees and Lazy M hands.

"Impressive," Faro said. "But it seems to me that there's about four times as many as is needed to float our fellows down for the attack."

"Their purpose is humanitarian as well as bellicose," Doc said. "Whoever's left standing after the fight gets loaded onto one of those, which is then shoved into midstream and allowed to drift out of our lives. We will probably lose some badly wanted men that way, but what the hell. A fight like this, it seems to me that taking prisoners is a waste of time."

"Reid is of a mind with you on that," Faro said, remembering the Ranger's comments in the Galveston bar, "but he don't figure to provide sea voyages for the prisoners he don't take."

After the initial shock of Doc's suggestion had abated, it had been accepted with surprising ease, and plans for the eradication of Louse Point had been formulated on the spot. It would be a two-pronged attack, with the rafts, manned mainly by Mal Holabird's employees and followers, drifting down and jumping ashores from the river, and the Lazy M hands, led by Reid, striking from the landward side; a signal flare from the rafts would assure that the two assaults were coordinated.

"I take it you'll be with me in the water-borne party," Doc said.

Faro nodded. "I will take boats, even such as them, over horses any time for getting anywheres, even to a fire-and-sword social," he said, "but I don't see why you are taking a hand and risking your neck."

"By sun-up tomorrow, dear boy, the work of dismantling Louse Point and making it as if it had never been will be under way. At some point in the proceedings someone is going to lift up a certain flagstone in the old fort to cart it away, and discover a wooden chest with the arms of the government of the Mexican Republic branded on its top. All things considered, I think that person had better be me. Aided by you, of course."

"And then what?" Faro asked.

"I have already suggested to Mr. McGree—who has very kindly offered me the hospitality of his ranch for a few days after the conclusion of this operation—that he could well use some of the stones for the fort for building material, even an ornamental courtyard if he wants it, especially as they have in any case to be removed so as to efface all trace of settlement.

The land party will be accompanied by several carts for that purpose, and I and you will see to it that we volunteer for the task of loading—and very definitely unloading at the other end—one of those carts. I need hardly say that it's share and share alike between you and me in the proceeds, even though you weren't involved in the original acquisition."

"I thank you," Faro said. "If I don't make it through the fracas tonight, it'll be a comfort to me in my last moments that I was at least trying to turn a few dollars on the deal."

They came upon Holabird, who was superintending the stowage of a large crate onto one of the already-completed rafts.

"What's that?" Doc asked.

"We don't have regular flares, for signaling to McGree's men when to hit them from the land side," Holabird said, "but I come across a crate of fireworks that got overlooked at the Centennial Fourth last year. They'll do fine."

He squinted downriver, toward where Louse Point lay. "You know, it's like old times, getting up a thing like this with Alex—and a funny thing that it's the same place, only elsewheres, so to say. Him and me had a long talk last night, and he finally proved to me that he'd got his money from his folks back East, and I proved to him that I'd got mine from the California land, so's we've laid to rest what's been cankering us all these years. Looks like that Mex gold has been on the bottom of the river all the time."

"Near it, anyways," Faro muttered.

"Huh? Anyhow, it's good to have that cleared up. Now Alex and me can join in this with a good heart. Like I said, like old times, or would be if only poor Locksley was here to make a third, like back then."

"Just consider that he's with you in spirit," Doc said blandly.

The rafts drifted silently with the current, tilting slightly from time to time as their steersmen poled them away from a snag or sandbank. Faro glanced behind him at the following fleet, patches of dark on the moonlit river.

"Nice of Holabird to give us places on the lead boat," he said to Doc. "That way, we're in on the fun from the beginning." He hefted the unfamiliar weight of the heavy revolver that had been issued to him, checked its cylinder to make sure it was fully loaded, and patted the pocketful of cartridges that was pulling his coat out of shape. He was as ready as he was ever going to be, which was, it seemed to him, not very.

Doc moved to the crate of fireworks and selected a stubby rocket attached to a long stick. "This should do nicely," he said.

"There much of a choice?" Faro asked.

"All sorts of things. Fountains, Roman candles, and so on."

While Doc wedged the rocket's stick into a chink, Faro rummaged in the crate and withdrew an assortment of fireworks, which he laid on the deck.

From the configuration of the river bank as he had seen it three nights ago he knew that they were approaching Louse Point, and the next bend in the river brought it into view.

The steersman poled the raft in toward the bank and the sloping beach that led up toward the settlement. It grated on sand, rocked, and was still. Men began jumping off the raft and onto land, pushing past Faro and Doc.

Doc struck a match and touched it to the rocket's fuse. There was a sputter, then a flare, and it soared into the night, leaving an arcing trail of sparks.

White light flooded the sky and lit the hovels of Louse Point and the derelict fort. A few seconds later there came a series of ear-splitting bangs; then a shower of red, white, and blue stars; and more bangs.

"I expect Reid and McGree's men will have seen that," Doc said with satisfaction.

Faro saw movement near the water's edge, struck a match and touched it to the fuse of a Roman candle he grabbed from the pile in front of him. Red and green balls of fire fountained from it with soft popping sounds. In their light, he saw a whiskered man on the beach, gaping at them and holding a rifle, which he slowly began to bring up. Faro aimed the firework's cylinder at him; the man yelled as a ball of fire took him in the shoulder, dropped his rifle, and ran off with his shirt smoldering.

"Novel use of artillery," Doc said approvingly. "You've got a talent for improvising, young Faro."

He and Doc stepped ashore and ran up the slope. Louse Point was finally reacting to the invasion, and yells and gunfire were erupting from all quarters of it. There was intense firing some distance ahead, which Faro took for the encounter between McGree's men and the startled defenders.

Drifts of powder smoke hung in the air, becoming heavier as the specially detailed fire starters splashed coal oil on the wooden buildings and torched them.

Faro and Doc pounded past the fort, then dove for cover inside it as gunfire pocked the dirt street around them. Faro looked out, and thought he saw Bob Holabird squinting over the sights of a rifle from the second floor of the saloon across the way. Whoever it was vanished as a fusillade from the invaders spintered the window frame.

A group of men erupted from the saloon, carrying rifles and shotguns. Faro squeezed off three shots at them; two men fell; the others dropped their weapons and shakily raised their hands.

That was close to the end of it, though for another quarter of an hour an occasional hardhead would open up on the invaders and have to be dragged from, or shot out of, his hiding place.

It was well before dawn, but everything burnable in Louse Point was now afire or had already been consumed, and there was plenty of light to see by as the survivors of the outlaw community were herded together in front of the fort.

Faro searched the motley crowd, and did not find either Bob Holabird or Jim McGree.

"Godamighty!" roared Alex McGree, standing beside him, powderstained and gripping a shotgun. "That woman there's got no clothes on at all. Suppose she come to lose 'em in the fighting, or what?"

It was Lucy, whom Faro had encountered on his first trip to Louse Point. "It's her uniform," he said. He scanned the crowd again, and saw the woman who had so notably contributed, if not to his luck, at least to his memories of the crap game in the building now smoldering behind her.

The rising sun was reddening the waters of the Rio Grande when the last of the dozen rafts carrying the former inhabitants of Louse Point were pushed out into midstream. The water behind them was littered with charred timbers and other debris from the wreckage of the settlement.

"There's stores of food and water on each one to last 'em a day or so," Mal Holabird said, "but they'll fetch up on one shore or t'other before then, for sure. Then they'll be some other town's problem, not ours. I wisht Bob was amongst 'em," he added venomously. "Son or no, I count him no kin any longer."

"I'd of liked to give Cousin Jim something to think on whiles he was excursioning on the river," Alex McGree said. "Such as a broken leg or a ear chawed off."

Mal Holabird sighed. "They weren't among the dead, so they must have cleared out, along with some of the others. One thing, Jim and Bob or no, it's a blessing to us to be seeing the last of that Louse Point crew."

"I wonder if any of 'em'll give that jaybird-naked lady a coat or so," Alex McGree said.

"They ain't a charitable bunch," Faro said. "I would guess she would have to earn it."

After Alex McGree dispensed coffee and sourdough biscuits from Owgooste's chuckwagon, the business of eradicating all trace of Louse Point began in earnest.

Faro and Doc, shirtless, sweated as they hoisted a heavy flagstone from the fort's floor onto the bed of a waiting cart.

"These are *heavy*, Doc," Faro complained. "Couldn't we get somebody to help us?"

"Considering what's under the next one we're going to take up, it'd be a case of those who help us helping themselves, I make no doubt. Now, get that crowbar under the edge and pry . . . that's it."

Doc gripped the underside of the stone, looked quickly around to make sure that no one was in immediate eye range, and lifted.

Faro looked down at what lay beneath the stone. "Is that it?"

Doc looked at him oddly. "Well, no, it's *another* Mexican Government strongbox that I buried here at the same time, just for fun. Now, help me get the son-ofabitch into that cart and out of sight!"

They both staggered under the weight of the chest —a burden that cheered Faro as he calculated what that weight of gold would buy. If Doc was right, his share of it would amount to seventy-five thousand dollars.

Once the chest, wrapped in Doc's coat and shoved into the corner of the cart, had been covered by two more flagstones levered from the fort, Doc summoned help for the remainder of the loading. When the cart was full, he and Faro drove it out of the rapidly vanishing Louse Point and along the winding track that led eventually to the Lazy M.

"So that clears everything up," Faro said. "I come through for Reid, so he's off my back now, and I am free as the little birds to go where I choose. And you have got that chest of gold that's been on your mind all these years. Times, I didn't see how it was to come about, but it appears to me that we have got the whole thing whipped and hung up to dry."

"Well," Doc said slowly.

"Well?"

"Well, we've got the chest, that's true. But next comes the question of leaving this garden spot of West Texas with it. I mean, Alex McGree, Mal Holabird, Captain Reid, and Marshal Pratt know very well what you and I have in the way of effects and luggage. When it comes time to mount the stage or take a downriver packet, questions will be asked for which we have no answers that do us one damned bit of good."

"Hey," Faro said faintly.

"The thing is, it is easier for a rich man to pass through the eye of a camel than it is for anyone to get out of San Bernardo or any burg of that size without being inspected and overseen, and inspecting and overseeing is just what we can't afford. A bigger place, there's a dozen or so ways to manage it, but we're not *in* a bigger place. We are, in fact, in deep shit unless and until we find a way of moving that chest without anybody taking notice of it."

Faro looked glumly over the rolling land in front of them. From somewhere to his left came the bawl of a longhorn; a stray, he supposed, missed in the roundup. . . .

"Doc," he said slowly, "I think I maybe got a handle on how we can work this. There is one question you got to answer first."

"And what's that?" Doc asked.

"Can you cook?"

Chapter 13

"I don't know about that, Mr. Prentiss," Alex Mc-Gree said dubiously. "You took a man's part in coming down on Louse Point, and it's for certain Captain Reid wouldn't have brought you into this unless you was a reliable man. But none of that really says that you got what it takes to be a trail cook."

Doc laughed lightly. "I assure you, Mr. McGree, that I have more strings to my bow than special assignments for the Texas Rangers. A man in his time plays many parts, as the Bard says."

Faro thought, true enough as far as you're concerned, Doc.

"As for serving as trail cook—well, you just ask Dick King next time you see him, or John Chisum, if J. L. Prentiss hasn't taken a turn as one of the best trail cooks they ever saw. *They'll* tell you."

So they will, Faro said silently, sitting with the two of them in McGree's parlor the day after the disinfection of Louse Point. But *what* they'll tell him is they ain't ever heard of no J. L. Prentiss. It's wonderful how Doc, whenas he wants to, can tell the strict truth but make it serve him as good as any lie.

"I have a hand with beans, stew, bacon, and coffee that you wouldn't credit," Doc went on. "No disrespect to the recent incumbent of the post, but when it comes down to the proof of the pudding or whatever, I'll venture that your hands will say there's no comparison with what Owgooste turned out. I've nothing pressing ahead of me, and it would please me to employ my talents in your service, especially as your need for a trail cook is a crying one. Also, I understand, the wages are good. Thrown in, you get the sure hand and gimlet eye of Mr. Blake, who would welcome the healthful rigors of the cowpoke's life for the ten or dozen days of the drive as a change from his normal endeavors."

Faro forced an appropriately earnest expression onto his features as he looked at McGree. He hadn't the least interest in poking cows, or whatever it was the trail hands did; but, if he were to accompany Doc, it would have to be that. The notion of using the chuckwagon to transport the gold to Alexa, the town where McGree's herd would be joined with the main one heading north, was too good to miss. Once in Alexa, there would be no problem in getting the chest—or at least the gold it contained—elsewhere.

"Well, it sounds all right, you put it like that," McGree said. "And the Lord knows, I need a cook bad. I haven't had the time to round up a full trail crew, so Mr. Blake'll be welcome. All right, you go tell Dora I've signed you on for the drive."

Far was surprised. "Dora?"

"Now Jim's not here, and good riddance to him, she

has took over some of the managing he got me to let him do. She is right now trying to round up what we need of a crew, so you'd best let her know there's two spots at least filled."

As they walked to the porch, where Dora had set up a table to serve her as an office desk, Faro said, "Doc, can you really cook?"

"Of course," the old man said, apparently affronted. "But you can refresh my memory on one technical point, if you will. Do you fry biscuits or boil 'em? I can never remember which."

"Oh, shit," Faro said.

Doc clapped him on the back. "Don't worry. Before the drive starts, I'll go into San Bernardo and have a chat with Owgooste. Doubtless he can fill me in on all I need to know."

Dora accepted Doc's self-proclaimed expertise without question and, after he had strolled off, turned to Faro. "Do you know much about trail herding?"

"Damned little."

"It's hard work, but easy enough to get the hang of for the most part, and Shorty's a top-grade trail boss, so he can show you the ropes. It's mainly a matter of keeping the herd moving at the right pace—not really driving them, but letting them drift in the right direction. You'll shift amongst riding flank, point, swing or drag, and of course take night duty when it's your turn. Most of the boys going along have enough experience to help you out if you run across anything you can't handle."

"Any others as green as me in the outfit?" Faro asked. "I would like somebody to keep an eye on as being just as like to make mistakes."

She gave him a sidelong glance and, for some reason, seemed to be amused. "I've signed on a young fellow, Steve's his name. He's never been on a drive before, either—he's hot to come along so he can learn the business, as he means to set up in ranching for himself some day."

"If he has got that far, having an ambition to make something of himself in this line, I could probably pick up some pointers from him as I go along," Faro said.

"I certainly believe you could," Dora said.

"Well, that was pretty good grub, I got to say," Faro told Doc. "If I didn't know you wasn't a cook, I wouldn't of knowed you wasn't a cook."

Doc beamed with pride. "Thanks. Owgooste gave me a tip when I was picking his brains in San Bernardo. Hash, he told me, is nothing much, though it's filling, unless you give it some snap. A few green chilies, chopped fine, makes all the difference, he said. So you liked it?"

Faro nodded. "More surprising to the tongue than your usual hash, for sure."

"How'd your first day as a trail hand go?"

"So-so. It was mostly a matter of riding kind of casual alongside the cows and seeing to it that they don't take the notion to get off the trail and go after grass whenas they ain't supposed to. I am some sore in the butt and some creaky about the shoulders, but on the whole I don't feel so bad. Worst of it was when Shorty put me to riding drag this afternoon—thass behind the herd," he added, pleased to display his newly won knowledge. "They kick up such dust that it coats a man inside and out, from izzard to eyeballs. And Shorty don't hold with carrying a flask of any good kind of dust-cutter, such as bourbon or rye. If I'd knowed this was a temperance outfit, I don't know but

158

what I wouldn't of had second thoughts about signing on."

"Come on round back," Doc said. He led Faro to the rear of the chuckwagon, pulled open a drawer and withdrew from it a flat bottle, which he handed to Faro. "One swallow, no more, to cut the dust," he warned. "I don't want Shorty coming down on me for getting you snollygostered. Also, that's got to last us until we get to Alexa."

He returned the flask to the drawer. "What else you got in there?" Faro asked.

"That's the possible drawer."

Faro eyed it. "Looks probable at least to me, maybe even certain sure."

Doc glared at him. "Means where they keep the things there'll be a possible need for—haircutting gear, bandages, remedies, sewing stuff."

"How is our own possible drawer taking the trip?" Faro asked. "The Mex chest, that is. Still in place and not suffering no fatigues nor distresses from the journey?"

"Just in front of the chuckbox, under my bedroll. The wagon listed to one side when we started off, so I hopped back and centered it dead between the wheels."

"Nice to know it is in good hands." Faro stretched and yawned. "This fresh air and outdoor exercise is starting to corrupt me. It's not much past sundown, and my thoughts is turning toward sleep. But I believe I'll mosey over and hunker down around the fire with the fellows whiles as they sing them plaintive laments the cowpoke is famed for."

To Faro's pleased surprise, the songs performed by the campfire dealt hardly at all with dogies, strays, coulees, mournful coyotes, or faithful ponies. Gamblers, sporting ladies, bloodthirsty outlaws, and steamship disasters formed the burden of the most memorable of them. One particularly bawdy ballad was sung in a pleasant, high tenor by Steve, the cowhand Dora had mentioned.

Steve, he thought, looked as though he should be singing in a choir instead of at a trailside campfire. The boy's wide-cheekboned, open face was trusting and innocent—deceptively so, Faro concluded, remembering the song.

Shorty hunkered beside him. "First day go okay?"

"Enough. Didn't let any cows get away nor run off weight nor get stung by rattlesnakes."

"Well, that's what we're here for. And listen, rattlesnakes don't sting, they bite."

"Whichever is their custom, none of 'em done it to any of the cows I was herding today," Faro said, yawning.

"Might's well get plenty of sleep tonight," the trail boss told him. " 'Cause you'll be powerful slim on that line of goods tomorrow. Your turn for night duty. Pairing you with Steve—second night out, not much chance of anything happening, so it makes sense to use the new men then, get them seasoned a little."

"I will sleep twice as hard now," Faro assured him, "to make up for what as I miss tomorrow."

During the noontime stop the next day, Faro and Steve were sent out to gather fuel for Doc's stove for the night's meal. As this stretch of the trail was open prairie, there was little or no wood to be found, and they were obliged to load up with buffalo chips.

"Shit!" Faro said, drawing his hand back as if it had been stung, which it almost had.

" 'S what we're after," Steve, a few yards away and

stooping to inspect a promising lode of manure, said.

"I mean, look at that murdering cocksucker there." Faro pointed at a jointed-legged, clawed horror with a whiplike tail that had been sheltering under the chip he had just picked up. "It near as perdition bit me."

"Scorpions don't bite, they sting," Steve said. "I should have told you, they like to hide under those things."

"Yes, you should of," Faro said. "I guess if I had to depend on a piece of dried shit for a roof, I'd be mean-minded, too."

Doc had finished ladling out the evening meal, and was looking worriedly at the cooking pot. "The thing about beans," he confided to Faro, "is that they're so damned small when they're dry, and you put a lot of 'em on to soak and boil, and then there's more than you can use. But I hate to throw them out."

Faro cocked his head and looked down the trail. "Heard something . . . yeah, there he is, rider, coming this way. Maybe you got a customer for some of them leftovers—could be, a fellow that's heard of your touch with the skillet and has got all into a sweat to come sample it."

The distant shape, surrounded by a cloud of dust, resolved itself into that of a black-clad rider on a white horse, and, on closer approach, was identifiable as Captain John Reid.

Doc welcomed the Ranger heartily and pressed a generously filled plate of food on him. "It's only beans and bacon," he said modestly. "But it's my boast that you won't get beans and bacon like that in the finest hotel in Austin or Fort Worth, nor even San Francisco or New York."

"No, I guess I wouldn't, at that," Reid said, after sampling Doc's offering.

"Well, thank you. What brings you along this way, Captain?"

"I hung around San Bernardo awhile, seeing if I could find what became of Jim McGree and Bob Holabird, but no luck. So I left today, and, as it's pretty much on my way to Austin, I thought I'd stop by and look in on you two. I would powerfully like to get hold of those two—they're too much of dab hands at scoundreling for me to feel easy while they're loose." The Ranger stared broodingly at his unfinished plate of beans and bacon. "Not sure what I could charge them with, but if I could clap the irons on them, I expect some thought would come to me on that."

"What we done at Louse Point, that might of made 'em see the error of their ways and sent 'em scuttering off frighted and resolved to sin no more," Faro said.

Reid shook his head. "They're not that kind. They are low and conniving and murderous and thieving and what else you like, but I'll say they've got guts. They'll go on playing their kind of game 'til they're done for for good and all."

Riding companionably alongside Steve on night duty, Faro felt impelled to make conversation. It might not be the custom among veteran cowhands, but Steve had no more practical experience of the trail than he. Steve, Faro supposed, was a good ten years younger than himself, maybe more—his smooth face suggested that he shaved very closely or had little need to shave at all. Fellows that age, it seemed to him, liked to be taken for men of the world.

"Looking forward to the end of the drive?" he asked. "A hot time in Alexa?"

"It'll be nice to be done with it," Steve said.

"Shorty was telling me there's a first-rate whorehouse in Alexa. I expect you'll be hightailing it there to get your ashes hauled, soon's we're paid off?"

"I don't think so."

"Well, a well-set-up young fellow like you, there's probably no call to pay for it," Faro said heartily. "It comes to humping, I expect you've had your share."

"About what I've fancied, I'll allow," Steve said, seemingly struck by a joke imperceptible to Faro.

He began to feel that he was doing a lot of work on this conversation and not getting very far. None of Steve's responses had led in any natural way to a further exchange, and he was having to dredge up each venture on his own. .

A boy like that, maybe he'd be more forthcoming if encouraged to boast about his conquests—a kiddish thing to do, but after all, Steve was a kid.

"How many women would you say you've had?" Faro asked.

The unexpected reply was an explosive snort of laughter. "I guess you wouldn't believe me if I told you," Steve said when he could control his voice, "so I won't."

"Well, don't, then," Faro said shortly, and fell silent, wondering what the hell he had said that was so funny.

Their horses plodded slowly around the sleeping herd. After a while Faro withdrew a thin cigar from the case in his coat pocket, started to light it, then called to his companion, "Smoke?"

"Ah . . . sure. Thanks." Faro handed over the cigar, which Steve inserted in his mouth with a certain awkwardness, then struck a match and held it to the tip. The cigar end glowed as the flame caught it and Steve drew hard on it.

The boy spluttered and choked, expelling the cigar from his mouth, then gave a shrill yell as it dropped, still burning, down the front of his shirt.

Faro cursed, edged his horse closer to Steve's, ripped the shirt down the front, sending buttons popping, and pulled the smoldering cigar away from his bared midriff. "You ain't supposed to inhale on a *cigar,* dummy! I would of thought that even a shirttail boy would know . . . that . . . you . . ."

He fell silent, staring at the wrenched-open shirt and what lay beneath it.

Steve smiled wryly, making no move to pull the edges of the garment together. "Well, I'm not a shirttail boy, as you can see. I got Dora to let me dress up this way and sign on as a hand, because I want to know all the ins and the outs of the cattle business, so we—"

"She tole me," Faro said. "So you're Stella Holabird. My."

"She told me about you too, Mr. Blake," Stella said. "Lots."

Chapter 14

Stella seemed to regard the matter of her identity and gender as not worth much notice as she jogged along beside Faro in the moonlight, surveying the sleeping herd. At any event, she did not bother to close her shirt, and Faro, glancing sidewise from time to time, was unsettled by the sight of her dark-tipped breasts jouncing in time to her mount's pace.

"Ain't it a little cool tonight?" he ventured after a while. "I could give you the loan of my coat, if you liked."

"Oh, it's warm, beautifully warm," she said. "The air's warm, the horse I'm sitting is warm, I'm warm all over."

"*So,*" Faro said, shifting his left leg as he suddenly became aware that a unexpected response to what Stella was saying, or doing, or looking like, had given him an erection which was painfully pinned between his thigh and the rim of his saddle, "you are figuring to learn the cow business?"

"That'll be Dora's end of it, really," Stella said. "She knows cattle, the raising of them and the marketing of them, and all that. Me, I'm interested in going in with Dora in the Lazy M when she inherits it, mainly because it's a way to make money while working with horses. I am just about a maniac for horses, I will tell you. The way they look, the way they smell, the feel of them when your legs are clamped around them . . ."

Faro agreed inwardly with Stella's statement that the night was not cool. It seemed to him to be damned hot; in fact perspiration was standing out on his brow.

"Well, but you're learning about the cow end of it, this trip," Faro said.

"I have to know *something* about it, after all. But even this part of it is more horses than cattle—the cattle just plod along as they're told by the men on the horses. A person on a horse, when they really fit right, why, that's something beautiful."

"If you say so," Faro said. "I am not much of a horse man myself, being more inclined to a well-sprung Studebaker wagon or a good Pullman car seat, where the horse doesn't come into it except as providing the hair on the upholstery."

"Dora said that you were more interested in throwing your leg over what has two legs than has four," Stella said with a demure tone that belied the content of her speech.

Faro reined his horse in. "Now, this horse shit—what I mean, this shit about horses—has now come to a *end*. You are beating around your bush, and mine, come to that, with that talk, and about Dora, and how warm the night is, and jouncing your tits at me while as we're riding along, and you know damned well what you're at and *where* I'm at, so why don't you just jump off your damned *horse* and set about it?"

"I thought you would never ask," Stella said, sliding out of her saddle and to the ground, and dropping her horse's reins so that he stood motionless with his head bowed.

Faro started to dismount, but Stella waved imperiously at him. "No, you stay there."

"Then how—"

Her fingers plucked at the waistband of her jeans, and the fly parted, letting the garment slide down. "We can't just stop here—we're on night guard. We have to keep moving around the edge of the herd." She rolled the jeans up, tucked them under her saddle, and padded toward him, wearing only the burst-open shirt and her flat-brimmed hat. "Give me a hand up."

Faro gaped at her, but reached down. She used his stirruped boot toe as a step, and swung across the saddle, facing him and wedged against the horn, driving him back against the cantle. She was muskily sweaty, and her thighs, resting on his, were taut. Her breasts, dark-tipped, but of no discernible color in the moonlight, swung inches away from his face.

"Hey," he said. He reached down and undid his trouser buttons and managed to extricate his erection from the prison of his trousers and bring it out into the night air. Stella clamped her thighs tighter around his, raised herself, and, with his hand and hers probing and guiding, found the entry spot and sank upon him.

"Whoo," Faro said. "That is nice. But—" He twitched one buttock, then the other. "—the way we are jammed into the saddle, I ain't positioned as to be very active, nor you aren't neither."

She gave a breathy chuckle, and he caught a whiff of the spice with which Doc had—perhaps ill-advisedly—garnished the evening's beans and bacon. "You don't think much of riding, huh? Mr. Blake, I will show you something about riding."

One bare heel kicked the horse's flank, and the startled animal jolted forward, imparting to Stella a quick jounce that made Faro gasp.

"He's pacing now," Stella said, eyes bright and mouth slack.

"That is good to know about." Faro slid his arms under the flapping shirt and held her tightly to him, feeling the soft squash of her breasts against his chest.

Her thighs flexed again, and her heel drummed a new signal to Faro's mount. "Cantering," she gasped.

The changed gait set her bouncing on him more vigorously, and he found it hard to wheeze, "I never rightly understood what that was."

Once more he was aware of her thighs clenching and of an order kicked to the horse. "Trot. . . ."

His only comment now was a throaty gurgle. The pounding of the horse he mounted, and the pounding thrust and slide of the woman who mounted him, her pelvic bone slamming into his at each stride with a force that might have been painful if it hadn't been so godawful *marvelous* had drained away his sense of himself, and he wasn't clear about whether he was on a horse or *was* a horse. . . .

"And gallop!"

"You two fellers find night duty hard going?" Shorty asked when Faro and Stella—now securely re-garbed as Steve—finished their tour just after sunrise and headed for the coffee Doc had waiting.

"Just fine," Faro's partner said.

"Takes something out of a man, I'll admit," Faro said. "But I would say I'm up to it."

168

Shorty said, "Well, it is good that you two green-horns got on so well on that duty; I'll pair you next time your turns come up. Did either of you hear some critter howlin' in the night? Could of been dreamin', but it seemed t' me that I heard somethin' like a coyote, only fiercer. Like maybe a painter or cougar —like them varmints, what it was I heard had almost a human sound to it, a howl as if some pore soul was goin' plumb crazy."

Faro coughed. "I'd of noticed something like that, I'd say. I believe you must of been dreaming, like you said."

The next six days of the drive passed with a reason-able lack of eventfulness, at least according to Shorty. A sudden hailstorm pelted them with ice balls up to the size of baseballs, killing two cattle and coming close to braining one trail hand. A group of dingy, mo-rose Indians equipped with shiny, assertive carbines demanded, and got, "wohaw"—tribute of cattle, with one of the least marketworthy culled from the herd for them. Quicksand at a river crossing claimed an un-wary calf.

"That is nothing at all to what it could be," Shorty said. "I have been on drives alongside which this is like a church supper, with peach ice cream to foller. The main thing is, we ain't had even the mutter of a stampede. Now, your stampede, that I hate like poison. A herd gets going like that, they will run off so much of their weight that there's no profit to 'em, not to mention the animals that strays and is gone for-ever. And then there is the occasional poor cowpoke that gets in the way and is tromped to tatters."

Faro squinted at the steel-gray sky that brooded over the broken country that lay ahead on the trail.

"You ever get any clues about when a stampede might be on the point of erupting?"

"Well, heavy weather like this, you want to start out watching for such."

Faro nodded.

"And, before they start in to running, they can kind of shift uneasy as they walk."

Faro glanced behind him at the forefront of the herd. How he was supposed to tell whether the cattle were "shifting uneasy" was beyond him. Even now, they gave a hard-to-pin-down impression of unease.

"And might so be, the eye is caught by a twitching of the horns on some critter that's got spooked and is tossing his head and sending out a glint of white from a-rolling of his eyeballs."

But that could happen any time, Faro told himself, without a stampede coming on, just as it was now.

"And then there is a kind of stir amongst 'em, as it might be a grove of cottonwoods starting to feel the force of a wind coming on, so as they commence to drift off to one side, bunching up and moving faster, until they're off and running and hell won't stop 'em."

"*Hey,* Shorty," Faro said urgently, sweat breaking out on his forehead.

The trail boss swiveled in his saddle, peered at the staring, agitated lead cows, packed close together and stumbling in a kind of crazy unison, groaned, "Shit, piss and morphodite corruption," pulled his revolver out, let off three shots, and bellowed, *"Mill, goddammit, mill!"*

Faro had been given some theoretical instruction in the maneuver of milling—circling in front of potentially stampeding cattle to break up the emotional and physical momentum that had brought them to that point—by Shorty and Steve/Stella, and was surprised to find that it worked pretty much as the theory had called for. The milling business had seemed to him to be about on a level with the scam of the Dutch kid poking his pinky into the dike.

But Shorty's crew, riding hard and fast, soon hazed the erratic bovines to the left, then left again, and once more left, until the leaders of what might have been the stampede had been turned in a narrowing spiral and stood, looking bewildered, at the flanks and tails of their fellows.

"Well, it is nice to know that a stampede ain't that much after all," Faro said, as Shorty detached him and the other hands from the now-rearranged and calmed herd.

The trail boss glanced at him. "Wasn't a stampede," he said, " 'cause we headed it off. You don't know how close we come to one. I do." He lifted one hand to pass it across his mouth, and Faro saw that it was trembling.

Shorty closed his eyes briefly, then opened them. "Heydy, Blake," he said, "let's us go get us a drink."

"Which there ain't none of on this drive," Faro reminded him, "by your express orders."

Shorty grinned at him. "Not since there has been chuckwagons and cooks and possible drawers has there been a chuckwagon cook without a bottle in his possible drawer. We will now go and get that cook to discharge of his plenty."

They rode toward where the chuckwagon stood, well ahead from where the herd leaders had been milled. Shorty snorted. "I would of hoped," he said, "that Doc would of had something hotted up to feed us after that, leaving aside his private stock, that we aim to dip into, but there's no smoke from the stovepipe. You suppose the old turd has decided it's time for a nap?"

And, in fact, they did find Doc Prentiss in what appeared to be a state of slumber—or would have, if it were not for the fact that his bed was the arid ground next to the wagon and that his face was a mask of blood.

Faro paused to lift his friend's wrist and test that its pulse still beat, verify that the copious flow of blood was the result of a scalp wound and raced into the chuckwagon.

Three-quarters of the supplies—meat, water, staples —were gone, though the special spices Doc had inherited from Owgooste were untouched.

Faro ran to the rear of the wagon, crouching under its arched canvas roof, and scrabbled under Doc's neatly tied bedroll, where the chest of Santa Anna's gold had been carried.

The space was empty.

Chapter 15

"Well, it don't make sense," Shorty said. "The dried apples and beans and flour and such truck is mostly gone, but we ain't but twenty-thirty miles from Alexa. Any of the boys could ride in there and back with whatever you'd need to fill out the cooking for the rest of the drive, and not be above half a day at it. When you've had a chance to rest up from that knock on the head you took, make out a list, and it'll be seed to all convenient and at the expense of Alex McGree. So, no, you and Blake do not get to go sniffing back to see if you can track the fellows that bushwhacked you and took the supplies."

Doc glared from beneath the bandages that covered his head. "The dastards who struck me from behind made off with some of my most secret and prize ingredients—without those, what was a masterpiece of cookery becomes mere fuel. I have to get them back."

"Fuel is what's expected from a trail cook," Shorty said. "And it all turns to shit in a day, anyhow. I ain't sparing you on that account."

Well, Doc, Faro thought, I will admire to see what kind of lie you feed Shorty to get us a chance at getting that chest back.

"Shorty," Doc said, "I will have to come clean with you. I personally do not care a turd and a half about replacing the supplies." He let his voice drop almost a full octave and looked solemnly at Shorty. "But when those men came upon me and struck me down unaware, leaving me to welter in my gore, they did not content themselves with taking such mundane goods as flour, bacon, coffee, dried apples, and so on. No, they rifled the very soul of a helpless man as he lay insensible, and took something that is to me about as precious as life itself."

Shove aside the ribbons and laces of the statement, and that's a fair description of a hundred and a half thousand dollars in gold, Faro acknowledged silently. This one of the times when he's going to go with the truth?

"For twenty years, until this afternoon, I wore, night and day, a locket fastened to a fine gold chain around my neck," Doc said in hollowly impressive tones. "Upon the surface of that locket was limned what was to me the fairest face that mortal man ever beheld. Secreted within it was a lock of hair—"

I can see that he ain't, and more power to him.

"—obtained at a time and in a place and manner that I beg you will not oblige me to recall. You will understand that there are circumstances that even a man steeled to the adversities of the world will find it too painful to dwell upon."

"Ain't there just," Shorty said faintly. Faro wondered what dime-novel visions of blighted romance, deathbeds and exhumations were dancing through the trail boss's head.

"And that locket, that very locket—would God there were a name better than 'locket' to express what it means to me!—was reft from around my neck by these soulless vandals. What my eyes beheld first upon awaking, what my fingers stroked for their last comfort before sleep welcomed me to a realm wherein that comfort was not needed, is now no more with me, but is become the subject of coarse jest as it is passed among profaning hands."

"My God," Shorty said.

"I wronged you when I tried to give you mundane and practical reasons to let me and Blake go after the villains," Doc said. "They were subterfuges, concealing a motive I dared not give—"

Back to the truth again, Doc? Faro thought.

"—but I must now make my appeal to your generous spirit. What those men took from me this afternoon, I must have, else I am no man. Let Blake and me hunt out the trail of these miscreants, and hazard what we may to retrieve a loss that will, if it be final, cloud my declining days."

Visibly affected by Doc's narrative, Shorty blew his nose between a clenched thumb and forefinger and said, "It might be a idea to let the herd rest up here a day, and put back a little weight. So I expect we can do without the two of you for maybe a day, day and a half. I don't expect that you'll be able to trail the varmints, but I can see that it'd set badly with you not to give it a try, for the sake of . . ." He gave Doc a sad, understanding smile and sketched a gesture at that part of his breastbone where a locket, had he worn such a thing, would have lain.

After the stocky trail boss had left the chuckwagon, Faro helped Doc from the bunk. Doc patted his head, winced and swore, removed the bandages and said, inspecting himself in a mirror fixed to one of the hoops supporting the canvas roof, "Just a gash. I doubt I'll need any stitches in it, which is just as well, since I'm the one around here that's expected to see to such, and I wouldn't fancy self-surgery."

"Doc," Faro said slowly, "that was a mighty affecting narrative you poured out onto Shorty, powerful and convincing. Was there *some* truth in any of that stuff about the locket?"

Doc glared at him. "What kind of asshole do you take me for?" he snapped.

The beginning of the trail of the chuckwagon thieves was not hard to find, once they had gone a few hundred yards from that vehicle.

Faro and Doc looked down at the debris in the matted grass below them. Heaps of coffee, flour and sugar lay there, next to the splintered remains of the Mexican chest.

"Clear enough," Faro said. "Once they were away from where they coldcocked you, they stopped to see what they had, and decided that the sacks was more useful for carrying the gold than for holding what they come packed with in the first place. Divvied up that way, the gold wouldn't be too much of a load, the way the chest was."

Doc stared at the trampled grass. "Looks to have been about six or eight of 'em," he observed. "Shouldn't be that hard a trail to follow."

Half an hour later, as they were circling to pick up the trail where it had been obscured by a rocky patch of ground, Faro glanced behind them at the ominously leaden sky. It seemed to him that he caught a flicker of motion in the distance, but it vanished. It could be a lone buffalo or antelope, he thought uneasily, and said nothing to Doc.

The trail, once recovered, led through rising, broken country and to the edge of a bluff. Faro dismounted and reconnoitered ahead, then came back to Doc. " 'S them. Down by a crick, seven men and a bunch of horses."

"Sure it's our bunch?"

"They was standing over some sacks and looking down at 'em," Faro said. "Enough of a pointer for me."

They left their horses ground tied and made their way halfway down the bluff, keeping to the shelter of the grass and scrub, then paused for another look at the thieves' camp.

"That big tall one," Faro said. "Ain't that—"

"Bob Holabird, yes."

"And I think I make out that Rick fellow, too."

Doc, crouching in the grass, whistled thoughtfully. "Two Louse Pointers, and above a hundred miles from there. . . . Young Faro, I'd figured that business at the chuckwagon for a chance encounter with a bunch of range pirates, but this puts a different complexion on it. There is something here that makes me uneasy."

"Weather alone would do that," Faro observed. The air had become oppressively still, and dark gray clouds churned against the paler gray that filled the rest of the sky. There was a tangy smell to the air that did not seem to come from the grass.

"It's more than that. If that crew came across us,

177

it's highly unlikely that it was by accident, and that I don't like at all."

"One thing," Faro said, looking again at the outlaw camp, "if Holabird and them with him got away from Louse Point, I'd of expected Jim McGree to be with 'em, as he wasn't among those killed or rafted out."

"I agree," Doc said thoughtfully. "He ought to be there."

"Only he ain't. He's here. Elevate, gents, *very* slow and careful."

Jim McGree arose from behind a clump of tall grass, with a rifle leveled at them. "Cousin Sam, it is good to see you again. Had a feeling we might be having callers, but I hadn't thought to find you amongst 'em. And the cook with the interestin' chest amongst his effects, too. I can see you've got a reason to trail us here, all right, and I'll admire to learn how it comes about that you got what Cousin Alex and Bob's old man has been at odds over these last thirty years. Advise you to make the yarn elaborate and crop-full of details, as how long it lasts is how long you both draws breath, pretty much. Downhill ahead of me, gents, hands in air."

At the camp, Doc and Faro were quickly disarmed, Bob Holabird dropping Faro's pistol-knuckleduster with a contemptuous frown, but holding the cut-down shotgun admiringly. "Was a man to set about the robbing of banks or such, this'd come in handy." He looked at Faro more closely. "Say, I know you."

"So do I," Jim McGree said. "He is my cousin Sam Jenkins from North Carolina."

Faro saw a stare of recognition from the man Rick, last encountered on the trail from Louse Point. It seemed to him that he and Doc would not find many friends here.

"He is also one of them that run us out of Louse Point," Bob Holabird said. "I recollect him, powerful clear, sighting at me over a gun barrel during the fight back there. Being a cousin give him any kind of claim on you?"

"Consider me a orphan and without family," Jim McGree said.

"I thank you." Bob Holabird flexed his knee, then drove his boot toe into Faro's crotch. Faro grunted and bent almost double, his head swimming and his hands cradling the site of his injury. At least I didn't scream nor pass out, he thought. Maybe that'll be some comfort to me in my last moments, which these seem to be.

Rick inspected the knife which had been taken from Doc. "That has the look of Pop Smollett's toad-sticker," he said. He looked up at Doc. "And you got the look of Pop Smollett, if it was in the nature of things that Pop was ever to shave and wash and have a change of clothes."

Holabird and McGree looked at Doc closely. "I will use shit for shavin' soap if it *ain't* Pop Smollett," McGree said.

"Seems to be a lot here that will divert us to know of," Holabird said. "I would say we done a good day's work, some supplies to chew on, four sacks stuffed tight as a sausage with gold, and now some good yarns for the entertainment part of the proceedings. Say on, Pop or whoever you are, and make the words good ones, as they're your last."

"Why all this about killing Pop and me?" Faro complained. "We come to get back what you took, as anyone would of, and you have stopped us, as anyone would of, so there ain't any reason I can see not to call it quits and move on. Seems to me, just knocking us out and leaving us to come to later on would fit the situation just as well, and save powder and shot."

Bob Holabird shrugged. "You're only getting it a day early, anyhow. Dawn tomorrow, we take out your trail crew to the last man, then move the herd on to Alexa ourselves. Jim here won't have no trouble handling the deal for old Alex, as he was the one meant to do it in the first place, and I misdoubt the Louse Point business has got known of there yet, at least it hadn't when we rode in there yesterday to see how things lay." He grinned. "A funny thing, Pop and Cousin, if them merchants in Alexa hadn't been so skinflinty, you'd not be here now. We was plumb out of food, not having been able to take away much in the way of funds and grub when you run us out of Louse Point, and went on ahead to see if we could get something on credit. But with them fellows it was cash on the line or no merchandise, so we had to raid the chuckwagon for what to eat. And then we come up with what took our minds right away from our bellies and into our pockets." He prodded a fatly packed sack at his feet.

"You want to tell us who we got to thank for this?" Bob went on.

Faro, facing toward the bluff, saw something stir at its crest against the angry gray sky, then the motion stopped. Something which had not been there before remained in his vision, a glimmer of white. A man with a lot of imagination and hope might persuade himself that it was the head of a tethered white horse.

"It seems to me, gentleman," Doc said, "that, with about a seventh of a million dollars in gold in your possession, that it wouldn't be worthwhile to slaughter the trail crew and do a couple of days' hard work just for the sake of the twenty thousand the herd'll fetch."

"Don't low-rate twenty thousand dollars," Jim Mc-Gree said. "Twenty thousand dollars ain't chicken feed. There's many a poor man would be glad to wake up tomorrer and find twenty thousand dollars in his poke."

"We planned it and we're going to do it," Bob Holabird snapped. "Any road, most of them, as well's you two, was in the raid on Louse Point, and it'll be some satisfaction to me to do some throat-cutting for that. You fucked up some mighty important plans, and it will take some blood to soothe my feelings about that."

His voice seemed shriller, and Faro felt a tension even more extreme than could be accounted for by the peril he and Doc were in. He wondered fleetingly if Bob's plans for wholesale massacre of the Lazy M crew would be changed by knowledge of the fact that his sister was one of them. He doubted it. Overhead, the sky was almost pitch-black, and seemed to writhe as if some giant hand were churning it.

"I say, cut the cackle and corpse 'em now," Jim McGree said, shifting his stance and staring uneasily. "We got any wonderments about what happened, we can make up the yarn to suit ourselfs later on."

"I got a big bump of curiosity," Bob Holabird said. "I mean to have 'em talk. We got the time."

"No you don't! In the name of the State of Texas, throw down your arms or die where you stand!" Faro, along with the rest, swiveled to see John Reid at the edge of the clearing where the camp lay, a massive revolver in each fist.

"Shit to that!" Jim McGree yelled, and scooped up Faro's shotgun. Before either he or the Ranger could fire, the eerie gloom of the afternoon was dispelled by a glare followed almost instantly by a crack that seemed to split Faro's eardrums.

Flashes and thunderclaps came in rapid succession, each instant of light catching the scene in frozen motion, like pictures in a magic-lantern show.

To Faro's astonishment, these tableaux depicted Jim, a look of frozen horror on his face, dropping the shotgun; the other outlaws doing the same, and then diving for the ground; and Reid still at the edge of the clearing, beckoning to him and Doc.

Faro scooped up his pistol and shotgun and ran. As he and Doc and the Ranger officer scrambled up the bluff, the celestial cannonade subsided.

"What the hell happened back there?" Faro panted. "Did you bluff them fellows out, or what? How come they throwed down their guns?"

"Your simple plainsman has the firm conviction that holding on to anything metal during an electrical storm is sure death," Doc said. "Makes the area a wonderful territory for lightning-rod salesmen. You wouldn't believe the business I did in that line in '73, until some misunderstanding came up about the quality of the materials. That lightning display was absolutely providential. I would say, Captain, that your bold play was backed by a pretty powerful ally."

"The only one the State of Texas needs, wants, or usually has," Reid said solemnly. Faro wondered briefly what the Ranger's daily dose of Sachem Onondaga's elixir had been.

"How'd you come to be there, anyhow?" Faro asked. They were almost to the top of the bluff, and he could see clearly the head of the Ranger's white horse, tethered to a stump. He realized that the sky was lighter by far now and that the lightning had died off, though the earth still seemed to tremble with distant thunder. He glanced behind them and saw activity in the outlaw camp: two men scrambling after them, and two more, mounted, making for a straggling track that angled up the incline.

"At Alexa, I heard that a pair sounding a lot like Jim McGree and Bob Holabird had been seen asking for credit to buy supplies. Thought it'd be a good idea to let you men know about that, came back to the herd, heard what happened, and came after you," Reid said briefly. He looked behind him, assessing the pursuit. "I don't like the idea, but I think we'll have to try to outrun them if we can get to our horses in time—no place here to fort up with any hope of holding them off. We can't count on a storm coming to our rescue again."

"I still hear thunder, though," Faro muttered, taking the last few yards of the slope in a rush and looking around for his and Doc's horses.

What he had heard was not thunder. Ahead of him, close, and coming closer each instant, a sea of wild-eyed longhorn cattle filled the prairie.

Faro now knew all at once—and deeply regretted the knowledge—why Shorty felt as he did about stampedes.

Chapter 16

Faro's first fevered impression had not been entirely accurate. The stampeding herd did not fill the prairie from horizon to horizon, but it occupied a good portion of it, and was coming straight at him, Doc, Reid, and the edge of the bluff.

The thunder of their hooves, the rolling glare of their eyes, and the flying foam that slobbered from their mouths was impressive and terrifying enough, but there was an extra touch to the picture that gave it a bizarre horror.

Wisps of blue flame flickered above the onrushing animals' backs, even flashing in an arc across the six-foot spans of their horns.

"What the hell is that?" he panted as he turned and ran, with Doc and Reid, to the waiting horses.

"St. Elmo's fire," Doc said. "Electrical phenomenon. The cause—"

"*Later,* Doc, thanks." Faro vaulted to his horse,

then jerked sideways as a bullet whined past his head. He looked down the slope and saw Bob Holabird taking aim with a rifle. He realized that Holabird, just as he had a moment before, must have taken the noise of the herd for thunder and be ignorant of the approaching stampede.

"Think we could ride acrost their front and turn 'em away from the bluff?" he called to Reid.

"Doubt it—we'll have enough to do to get away from 'em ourselves. Besides, slope's not so steep that many of 'em's likely to get killed or hurt." Reid urged his horse ahead along the brow of the bluff, riding toward where the herd seemed thinnest.

"But them fellows down there will get trampled all to shit," Faro said.

"Well, *yes,*" Reid said cheerfully. His powerful horse surged ahead, and Faro and Doc pounded after him.

The first animals were already plunging over the bluff and downslope when the three men approached the far edge of the runaway herd. Faro glanced behind him and saw the two riders who had been making their way up the bluff appear at its top—for only an instant of bewilderment and shock before the tide of cattle reached and overwhelmed them.

Faro jinked his horse to avoid the charge of a maddened steer which plunged by inches behind him and vanished over the edge of the bluff. He felt the heat of its passage, as though it had been powered by a coal-fired boiler. Then they were onto open prairie, away from the stampede.

As the last of the cattle began their descent of the bluff, Shorty rode up to them. "Glad to see you fellers wasn't caught. The bastards spooked when the lightning come, and there wasn't a thing to do once they was going but let 'em run it out. They won't go far, I expect, but we'll be all night roundin' 'em up again, and the Lord knows how many pounds of been run off of 'em. I better lay over another day or so and let 'em feed up some more."

He looked morosely toward where his charges were scattered, then turned back to Doc. "You find them fellers that made off with your locket?"

"What f—oh, yes," Doc said. "The locket. Ah, yes, we encountered the miscreants, but, before I could force it from them, we were overwhelmed by the stampede, and the villains perished to a man, I am sure. Whether it can be retrieved from the ghastly scene of their richly-deserved deaths, I know not, but I propose to try."

"When the herd's back together termorrow," Shorty said, "they'll be restin', so some of the boys'll be free. I'll have 'em lend you a hand."

Doc shook his head sadly. "I appreciate the offer, but this is for me a sacred quest. My old friend Faro and I will undertake the grim task ourselves. Whatever the outcome, I would wish to be alone with the memories of one who—memories, I will say, to particularize no further, that he and I alone share."

Indeedy yes, Faro thought. Memories of a hundred fifty thousand in gold, now scattered and trampled and mixed in mud, we do share those. Sacred quest, for sure. . . . He looked admiringly at the old confidence man.

Reid stirred. "I'll be off now," he said.

"See you in Alexa?" Faro asked.

The Ranger shook his head. "The mayor there knows me, and when I was in town this time, he kept pestering me to resign my commission in the Rangers and sign on with them as town marshal, the post being

187

open now owing to a disagreement with some hard-cases the last one lost. I was pretty short with him when I had to make it clear that my 'no' had to be taken as final, and I'd as soon not go through there again until we can be on friendlier terms. Also, the drugstore there doesn't stock Sachem Onondaga's Bitters, so I'd as soon cut across country to some place that might."

Doc coughed. "In the absence of the tonic you mention, I would recommend the substitution of Chief Tonto's Silver Remedy. The ingredients may vary from your favorite, but I am assured that the general effect is the same."

"Chief Tonto's Silver?" the Ranger said. "Thanks, I'll remember that. *Adios.*"

With a wave of his hand, he rode into the distance, silhouetted against the clearing sky.

"Making in all?" Faro said.

Doc, sitting beside him at the edge of the creek, surveyed the piles of neatly stacked gold coins, freshly washed of mud—and often worse—representing the total of what they had painstakingly and unpleasantly grubbed from the torn ground that had been the outlaws' camp. "Three thousand, seven hundred forty," he said bitterly.

"My, my," Faro said. "Even allowing for the likelihood that there's as much still churned up and ground in, that we ain't going to get without ditch-digging tools, that's not but what was in one sack, and the smallest at that."

"Now," Doc said, "it could have been eight men that we found the bodies of . . ."

"Or it could of been seven. Given how them cattle

went through here and what they done, there ain't no way of making sure, is there?"

Doc grinned. "It does make sense. Imagine that, Jim looking up and seeing those steers coming down on him, and with enough speed and nerve to throw those sacks over a horse and hightail it out ahead of them. You've got to hand it to him—Reid was right when he said those fellows had guts."

"He was about Bob, for sure," Faro said with a shudder, remembering the state Holabird's corpse had been in when they had found it.

"If he did get away with it, interesting to speculate how he'll use it. I hope he keeps hold of it, maybe invests it in something so it grows."

"Why the *hell* would you hope that kind of thing for that sonofabitch?" Faro asked.

Doc smiled broadly. "Because if Master Jim does prosper, there's a chance that I'll run across him again, in one or another of my guises. And I will take it all away from him, penny by penny."

"How?"

"Whatever method suits the circumstances: fake stocks, the wire room, a land deal, bribing a Congressman. There'll be something that'll do the job," Doc said.

"Makes you so sure of that?"

Doc rose and began distributing his share of the gold coins about his person. "Because, my dear boy, they say, and they're right, that you can't cheat an honest man. By that reckoning, Jim McGree should be about the easiest mark in the world!"

"Well, at least we got paid the going rate for the trail drive," Faro observed as he and Doc strolled down Alexa's Main Street three days later.

"Better," Doc said. "Half a month's wages for only thirteen days' work."

"Fifteen dollars for me and twenty-five for you ain't going to go very far," Faro said acidly. "I was getting to enjoy that style of work, but it don't pay well, so I guess the benefits of fresh air and exercise ain't worth it."

"Considering what we went through to get the rest of it," Doc said, "Louse Point and the stampede and all, I don't know that we earned that eighteen-seventy each any easier. I am figuring to head out north on this afternoon's stage to see what might be going on in Dodge and such places. You want to come along?"

Faro shook his head. "No, thanks, Doc. I believe I'll stick around here and rest up, maybe put on some weight, like Shorty had the herd do. That young fellow, Steve, is laying over, too, and it comes to me that I could economize by sharing a room with him."

"Suit yourself. Good luck, then, boy." He extended his hand, and Faro shook it. "Take care, young Faro," Doc said. "This has the name of being a tough town —that's why they wanted that Reid as a marshal. Heard at the barbershop this morning that they got themselves a new one, tough, a real hard article, coming in tomorrow or so."

"That so?" Faro said. "Well, I will keep my nose clean and be a total and law-loving citizen whilst I blamelessly enjoy Alexa's amenities and show young Steve a thing or two about life. No marshal, tough whatsoever he be, will be able to look on me as anything but blameless and upright, and looking to him for the upholdment of the law. That Louse Point, I'll tell you, gave me a think or two concerning the legalities—if I got to bend them from time to time, fine, but it is a comfort to know they're there. If I see this marshal, I will clap him on the back and buy him a drink. A beer, anyhow," he added cheerfully.

"Do that," Doc said. "Just ask for Marshal Ben Schofield."

"*And* then again, Doc," Faro said after a long pause, "there is things to be said for seeing what's doing in Dodge!"